"I would hel

The words were out of his mouth before he'd had time to think, but once they registered, he decided the idea wasn't so crazy. If he was going to follow through with the two of them getting along and putting the past behind them, he might as well jump with both feet.

Curiosity and concern mingled in the depths of her distractingly beautiful green eyes. Maybe even a bit of fear. "Why?"

"Why not?"

It seemed easier to answer that way than to tell her the truth. There was one thing he'd never seen his father and mother do—make amends. Forgive. Move on. Therefore that was exactly what Hunter planned to do.

And this way, when Rachel did her next disappearing act for the job she wanted and came back to visit her family, she and Hunter would be able to get along. Wish each other well.

She studied the toes of her camel boots as though they held the answer to all of the world's problems. "It was nice of you to offer, but I can't accept."

Couldn't? Or wouldn't?

Jill Lynn is a member of the American Christian Fiction Writers group and won the ACFW Genesis Contest in 2013. She has a bachelor's degree in communications from Bethel University. A native of Minnesota, Jill now lives in Colorado with her husband and two children. She's an avid reader of happily-ever-afters and a fan of grace, laughter and thrift stores. Connect with her at jill-lynn.com.

Books by Jill Lynn

Love Inspired

Falling for Texas
Her Texas Family
Her Texas Cowboy

Her Texas Cowboy

Jill Lynn

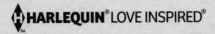

HARLEQUIN® LOVE INSPIRED®

Recycling programs
for this product may
not exist in your area.

LOVE INSPIRED BOOKS

ISBN-13: 978-1-335-50949-9

Her Texas Cowboy

www.Harlequin.com

Printed in U.S.A.

Being confident of this very thing,
that he which hath begun a good work in you
will perform it until the day of Jesus Christ.
—*Philippians* 1:6

To the God who makes all things possible—
even books that feel impossible—
all glory and honor to You.

T, S & L—I'm so thankful home is
wherever we are together. There's nowhere I'd
rather be than with the three of you.

To my editor, Shana Asaro—Thank you
for your hard work and dedication.
Your wisdom and guidance is priceless to me.

Chapter One

Time to make a break for it.

Rachel Maddox beelined for the back of the church and the sanctuary of the outdoors.

In the last five minutes, since the service had ended, she'd been cornered by three well-meaning women. Each had wanted to know every detail of her life since she'd left town six years ago. The first had wrinkled her nose with confusion when Rachel mentioned her future plans, instead—moving to Houston for a high school guidance counselor position she hoped to get. As though she hadn't understood Rachel's desire to hightail it out of Fredericksburg as quickly as possible.

The second had been hard of hearing, and she'd asked what perfume Rachel was wearing. Since the answer was none, she'd tried to change the topic, but after numerous requests, she'd finally piped up and said, "It must be my deodorant," at a volume high enough to have several confused glances swing in her direction. *Sigh*.

Number three had questioned why she wasn't married yet—as if twenty-four equaled old maid status—

all while giving her a pointed look that said she knew exactly why. Rachel had been reduced to a teenager in that moment—as though her old mistakes, attitude and poor decisions were strapped to her back for the world to see.

Ouch.

The nosiness was just another reason she wanted out of this small Texas town she'd grown up in. Rachel had this strange desire not to live in a place where she'd been a mess. It was time to start somewhere new, and just as soon as she got the job in Houston, that's exactly what she planned to do.

She dodged around two older gentlemen, the need to escape causing her throat to constrict.

Rachel had grown used to anonymity over the last few years. She attended big churches where nobody knew her name and lived in a city where people didn't stop her at the grocery store to chat about the weather or to ask how her sweet nephews were doing. This town was suffocating her, and she'd only been home a few days.

How was she going to survive a month or two?

People parted before her, and she clicked along in her sleeveless blue pencil dress and strappy brown wedges, the taste of victory and freedom spurring her forward.

When a little girl darted out in front of her, Rachel screeched to a stop. Tiny strawberry-blond pigtails bounced on the top of the girl's head like small antennae. Based on the fact that she roamed the sanctuary without a parent in tow, Rachel assumed she must be escaping, too. They were kindred spirits.

She only looked to be around two years old. Too small to continue her romp of freedom alone. So much for her escape plan. Rachel knelt down, gently touching the child's arm. "Where's your mama, sweetie?"

"Mama." The girl's face broke into a smile. Adorable. Not exactly helpful, but definitely cute.

"Should we go find her?"

The tot's head bobbled. Rachel attempted to take her hand, but the little girl didn't budge. When Rachel opened her arms, the girl came right to her. No stranger danger with this one. Rachel scooped her up and stood, a sweet orange scent reminiscent of the push-up treats she used to eat as a kid tickling her senses as she scanned the space for a harried mom. None appeared. Hmm. She couldn't exactly drop the toddler in the lost and found.

And then, instead of a worried mom, she saw a man steaming toward her. One she knew well. Hunter McDermott. Never fun to run smack-dab into a past mistake. And to think, she'd been so close to making a getaway.

He stopped in front of her, and to her surprise, the little girl lunged into his arms. Hunter…had a daughter? Rachel hadn't heard that he'd married. But then, when her sister-in-law, Olivia, started telling her about local news, Rachel often tuned out.

"Rach, I didn't realize you were home." Surprise laced his voice, joining the quirk of his eyebrows. The fact that he'd used her nickname seemed lost on him. "Sorry about that. Kinsley's a bit of an escape artist."

"It's okay. I completely understand." But, then again, he should know that. Hadn't he been upset with her for making a break for it six years ago?

Time had barely aged him. Hunter had never lacked in the spine-tingling looks department, yet he managed to pull it off without any effort. Of course he'd wear a casual, short-sleeved plaid shirt and jeans to church along with cowboy boots. His cropped, dark-blond hair looked as though he'd shoved a hand through it, glanced in the mirror and shrugged. He somehow managed to look laid-back and dangerous all at the same time. Two good words to describe the man who'd trampled all over her heart before she'd left for college. Though he would probably claim she'd been the wrecking ball.

"You home to see your family?"

"I just finished grad school and now I'm staying here while waiting to hear about a high school guidance counselor position I'm hoping—" *planning* "—to get in Houston." Rachel had already filled out tons of paperwork and done one interview over Skype.

His jaw hardened, brow pinched. "Sounds like you plan to escape as fast as you can."

She strived for polite, resisting the temptation to roll her eyes at the jab. She'd matured over the years, hadn't she? She could handle an adult conversation with Hunter. "Is this your daughter?"

"Kinsley?" Hunter lifted the girl higher, grinning at her. The softening of his face caused a tightening in her chest. Once upon a time she'd craved that smile of his as much as oxygen. "No. She's my niece. Autumn's oldest. She's pregnant with their second. I'm not married."

The words dug like a knife and twisted. He could have added *because of you* to the end, just to make the torture more complete. It was true he'd asked her to marry him once. But they'd been young—way too young. And she'd wanted out. A chance to start over where she hadn't been an immature teenager. Time to pursue her dreams. Was that so wrong?

Rachel still had hopes and aspirations that didn't involve this town. After high school, she'd gone to Colorado for college and concentrated on her studies. Now she planned to focus on her career.

Houston was four hours away. Close enough that she could see her nephews whenever she made the drive and yet far enough that she could start fresh. Rachel wanted to be in Texas and somewhat close to her brother, his wife and their kids—they were her only immediate family, since their parents had passed away when she'd been thirteen. But she didn't want to live in Fredericksburg. She enjoyed bigger cities. Liked everyone not knowing what she was up to and then gossiping about it.

For instance, just the fact that she was conversing with Hunter would cause a ripple that would echo across the smooth surface of this town.

"Hunter. Rachel."

Their heads both snapped in the direction of the voice. The associate pastor, Greg Tendra, approached, sporting a grin that wasn't mirrored on Hunter's face or hers. He wore a green dress shirt tucked into black pants and no tie. The man was an inch or two shorter than Rachel, with raven curly hair, and the smell of spicy aftershave wafted with him.

"I'm glad to see you two have met."

A laugh almost escaped from her throat, but she managed to stem it before it burst out. Being new to town, Greg obviously didn't know any of the history between Hunter and Rachel. Fine by her. What had happened between them would stay in the past, as far as she was concerned. She didn't need to confess to the pastor that they'd once had a vibrant relationship that had turned toxic. That when she did come home, she and Hunter couldn't manage more than a few minutes—seconds, really—of stifled surface-level conversation.

But why would Greg care if she and Hunter had met? Unless...

Her stomach plummeted to her cherry-red-painted toenails. No. It couldn't be. Dread crawled across her skin even as she tried to talk herself out of the idea.

"You're my leaders for building the float with the youth group this summer. The brawn and the brains." Greg's face wreathed in a teasing smile as he glanced from Hunter to Rachel, and her world crumbled around her. She'd agreed to do one thing while home—help the youth build a float for the Independence Day parade. She'd said yes for a number of reasons. It would give her something to do while home. It would even look good on her résumé, and she needed all the help she could get to land this job. But mostly, she loved teens. All the snarky sides of them. Just like she'd been, way back when.

But she hadn't realized the opportunity would come with Hunter attached.

She was supposed to work with him? Rachel wasn't sure how to handle that. She only knew her plans remained the same: get the job she wanted and break out of this town. And just like the last time, she couldn't let Hunter McDermott stand in her way.

Hunter's ears were ringing. They felt like Kinsley had taken a pot and a pan and banged his head between them. His niece squirmed in his arms, and he realized that during Greg's revelation, he'd been squeezing her pretty tight. When he spotted his sister, Autumn, talking to someone about ten feet away, Hunter placed Kinsley on the ground. A soft pat on her diapered bum had her scooting off toward her mom. When he was satisfied she'd been captured by his sister, Hunter turned his attention back to the strange turn of events happening in front of him.

By the look of pure shock on Rachel's face, Hunter imagined Greg hadn't informed her of who the other leader would be, either. He must have assumed they didn't know each other. He couldn't be more wrong on that account.

Would Rachel run now? She was certainly good at it.

Hunter winced. When had he turned so bitter? He was morphing into his father, and he didn't like it.

He could be a gentleman and back out of helping. Rachel was the teen whisperer, not him. He was pretty much the brawn, like Greg had joked. Hunter had been asked to help with the float because he had a truck and a flatbed trailer. Two things that were needed. He'd agreed to help because he loved the youth group. He'd spent plenty of time there as a kid. It had become a safe place for him after his mom left, and he wanted to give back to that. He still did, but how could this ever work?

"We're thankful to have the two of you helping. I honestly wasn't sure what we were going to do. But now that we have you both, crisis averted." Greg's sigh of relief told Hunter even more than his words. Hunter only knew Greg a little, but the man had been thrown into numerous roles at the church, even having to cover for the youth pastor who'd left unexpectedly.

So much for Hunter's idea of quietly disappearing. He wouldn't leave the church or the kids abandoned like that. Building the float had been the highlight of a few of his summers, too. It was tradition, and he remembered how much he'd looked forward to it.

Hunter sought Rachel's eyes, wishing he could read her like he used to be able to. Back when they'd been inseparable. When she hadn't looked at him as if her dog had just died and he was to blame. What was she thinking? "Didn't you say you were here waiting on a job?" How would she have time for something like this? How long would she actually be home?

"I am." She toyed with a gold R pendant that hung on a slim chain around her neck, her fingers a stark white. "The school is doing more interviews and then waiting for a decision from the board. It might take a month or two."

"We'll take you as long as we can have you," Greg chimed in.

That made one of them. Been there. Done that.

Greg's hand momentarily rested on Rachel's arm after his comment, and Hunter fought annoyance at the man and at himself for caring. What Rachel did or didn't do wasn't any of his business and hadn't been for a long time. But Greg was young—maybe just a few years older than Hunter—and not blind. Rachel was beautiful. Tall, with straight, light-blond hair that landed inches past her shoulders and mesmerizing green eyes. He'd always been partial to the subtle smattering of freckles on her face that he knew she despised.

Her beauty hadn't been the reason Hunter had once wanted to hold on to her, but it had been a perk to look at her pretty face every day and see her smiling at him as though he made the stars shine at night. Only he hadn't been enough to keep her here.

A quick glance at the ring finger on her left hand

told him she wasn't engaged or married. He assumed he would have heard if she was. Lucy Redmond—Olivia's sister—used to feed him tidbits of information about Rachel. But even Lucy's optimism couldn't overpower the messy past between Hunter and Rachel or the fact that they wanted completely opposite things.

Rachel had always had one foot out the door of this town, and his life was here. Hunter should have known to leave well enough alone when they were younger and not pursue a relationship with her, but she'd been hard to resist.

Greg had continued talking, and Hunter forced himself to concentrate on the conversation. "The search for a youth pastor probably won't wrap up until the end of July. But with you two handling the float, we only have the lock-in to cover, which I'm heading up, and then we'll hopefully have a new youth pastor starting in August or September."

The man looked pleased as punch. Hunter didn't know what to feel. For so many years, he and Rachel had avoided each other. They'd never dealt with what had happened between them. It had just been easier to sweep their past under the rug. He blamed her for so much, and he was just as sure she held him responsible for what went wrong.

And now he sounded like his father—stuck. Unable to move on.

If there was one thing Hunter wanted more than a quiet, content life of ranching, it was to not turn into his dad. He would do just about anything to avoid following in his old man's footsteps.

The three of them talked for another minute about when the float building was scheduled to start—this

Wednesday. And what time—seven o'clock. Then Greg split off to catch up with someone else.

"I—" Rachel looked as though she'd witnessed a terrible car accident, a bit of green dusting her face. "I should go find my nephews and Cash and Liv. They're probably waiting for me."

She didn't leave him any time to respond before she headed for the front doors of the church. Should he follow her? Make sure she was okay?

Nah. She wouldn't welcome his intrusion.

Hunter watched her burst out into the sunlight, angst churning in his gut. The memories with Rachel flooded back, fast and furious. Before their relationship had gone so wrong, it had been good.

But what had stood between them six years ago still stretched between them now. That and a lot of hurt.

Hunter refused to turn into his father and grow resentful, holding on to the past. Which, if Rachel and Hunter were going to be working together with the youth, meant one thing. The two of them were just going to have to learn to be friends again.

Whether she wanted to be or not.

Chapter Two

Ouch. Rachel jolted awake when her elbow met the wooden side of her nephew's fire truck bedframe. She rubbed the spot and stared up at the ceiling.

The house Rachel had grown up in—where her brother, his wife and their two boys now lived—only had three bedrooms upstairs and a small office downstairs. Her four-year-old nephew, Grayson, occupied one bedroom, and Ryder, who was just a year old, had a slightly smaller one. Cash and Olivia were in the master. There was no guest room, which meant that, with her added into the mix, Gray was sleeping on Ryder's floor so she could have his room. He currently considered the situation "very cool" and liked "camping" every night, but that wouldn't last forever. Certainly not for the month or two she'd be home. And while she didn't mind sleeping in a twin bed the shape of a fire truck, she was willing to live somewhere else and give Cash, Olivia and the boys their own space back. Except that, with her limited amount of time in town plus the fact that she should be saving money, she wasn't sure how to solve the space dilemma.

"Auntie Rach, watch out, the stampede is coming!" Grayson tore into the bedroom and jumped onto the bed with her, causing air to rush from her lungs.

"Grayson Warren Maddox, I told you not to wake her." Olivia paused in the doorway to Rachel's temporary room. She blew a wayward hair from her forehead, looking a little frazzled for eight o'clock in the morning.

Rachel's sister-in-law had aged well in the years since she'd met and married Cash. She wore khaki shorts and a navy blue T-shirt, her long mocha hair pulled into a ponytail. Even without makeup, she was striking. But more than her outside beauty, she was tender and compassionate with enough snark to make her likeable. The sister Rachel had never had. When Rachel had been in high school, Olivia had been her volleyball coach. She'd made a huge impact on Rachel and mentored her at a time when she'd been missing her parents and floundering.

"Sorry, Rach. Gray needs to get dressed and I had planned to sneak in and grab a few things without waking you. But it seems our boy had a different idea."

Rachel captured Grayson and tugged him close, holding him in a tight grip that made him squirm and giggle. "It's okay. I was up and hungry, and I love to eat little boys for breakfast."

He squealed and tried to get away while she smacked a kiss to his chocolate hair that still carried the sweet, fruity smell of kiddo shampoo from last night's bath.

"Auntie Rachel, will you take me riding?" When those hazel eyes peered up at her, Rachel didn't stand a chance of saying no. Not that she wanted to. Part of her plan for the summer was to help Liv with the kids. If she was home waiting on a job, she could at least lend a hand. She'd already finished all of the requirements needed by the State of Texas in order to be ready for the new opportunity. Which meant now she needed to occupy herself while playing the waiting game.

"Yep. Just let me get dressed. Can't ride in our pajamas."

Grayson's eyes lit up. "But that would be cool."

Within a half hour Rachel had eaten a bowl of cereal and downed a cup of coffee. Now she and Grayson were saddled up and headed out. He looked so happy, sitting in front of her in the saddle, mini cowboy hat on his head. Her heart just about gushed out all the love it held. She really, really adored her nephews. They were one plus in being home this summer.

The two of them meandered out on the ranch, stopping to visit with Cash and a few of the ranch hands before riding to the east edge of the property.

Rachel had forgotten about the old house that popped into view. It had been part of a ranch that had gone under decades before, and her parents had bought the land as an addition to the Circle M. She remembered a story about a skirmish between her dad and Hunter's, as they'd both wanted the property flanked by their two spreads. Her father had won the tussle, and she and Hunter had grown up on neighboring ranches.

Not that the McDermotts cared about this small slip of ranchland anymore. They were like land barons. They'd snatched up a number of smaller ranches over the years and now had a massive operation.

She directed Bonnie, the sweet mare they were riding, toward the house. A grayish hue tinted the white paint, as though the siding had given up fighting against the Texas sun years before. It looked deserted. No recent tire tracks. The grass around it was unruly and long.

Strange. Before she'd left for college, various ranch hands had rented the small house or negotiated living there as part of their pay. She didn't know what Cash did with it now.

Movement to the east caught her eye. A man on a horse crested a hill on the McDermott ranch. Too far away to tell for sure who it was, especially with the cowboy hat, but the build could definitely be Hunter's.

"Can we get down and look around?" Grayson questioned.

"Sure!"

Gray looked at her a little funny, and why wouldn't he? She'd just shown a lot of excitement for poking around an empty house. But if it would help her avoid a run-in with Hunter—if that was him—she couldn't resist.

Rachel still couldn't believe the two of them were in charge of building the float with the youth. That would have been useful information to have when Greg had asked Rachel to help. Since their conversation at church yesterday, she'd gone over and over the situation, and she couldn't see an escape route. She'd committed, and she wasn't going to back out and leave the church strapped. Besides, she wanted to work with the teens. This would be a great opportunity to show the town she'd changed—that she wasn't the same immature girl she'd once been.

Rachel wanted people to see her as who she'd become. Not the queen of bad decisions. A crown she'd once had the monopoly on.

She and Hunter would just have to function around

each other. If they limited their interactions to Wednesday nights and the occasional sighting at church, Rachel would be out of here and on to her new life in no time.

Bonnie meandered to a stop on the west side of the house, and Rachel and Grayson slipped down from the saddle. Her nephew was more at home riding than most adults she knew. Definitely her brother's child. When they'd been kids, Cash had always been out working with the horses, doing anything mechanical, helping move cattle and bumming around the ranch with Dad, even at a young age. The memory coaxed a smile. She was thankful the ache of missing her parents had lessened over the years, though it always remained with her.

What she wouldn't give to be able to go back for one day and tell them how much she loved them.

Gray had already taken off around the front of the house, so Rachel secured Bonnie to the hitching post and trotted after him. The kid only had one speed—fast.

"Can we go inside? Maybe we'll find a snake!" He'd already climbed the front steps and now stood on the small wooden porch. He tossed his hat on the stair railing, leaving a thick head of mussed brown hair visible. "Or a black widow spider. Or a tarantula." His excitement increased with each suggestion, while Rachel's mind screamed, *Turn around. Fast.*

She peeked through the front window. Papers, a turned-over chair, clothes and some other random items littered the floor. On the front porch, an abandoned wooden swing hung by only one chain. The other side scraped eerily against the floorboards in the slight breeze.

No one lived here. Not at the moment.

"We can try, bud, but I would assume it's locked."

Rachel attempted to turn the knob, but it didn't twist. Mostly to prove to Grayson that she'd tried, she shoved on the door with the palm of her hand. Amazingly, it eased open. The latch must have been broken. She pushed the door open wider, and it creaked and groaned as though arthritis crippled its hinges.

Before going inside, she gave the porch a good hard stomp, just in case any critters did live inside. Ignoring the creepy feeling that a spider was about to descend on her head, she took a tentative step inside. It smelled... musty. But daylight streamed in through the windows, illuminating a basic, but surprisingly roomy space. A small bedroom was visible through an open door to the right, and the kitchen area held a few cabinets and an avocado-green stove. An older fridge—the kind that would probably go for megabucks as vintage on eBay— had the doors propped open. Thankfully the contents had been cleaned out before it had been left unplugged.

"Whoa." Grayson had followed her inside and now stood next to her, thumbs hooked through his belt loops as he studied the room. "This could be my fort. I'd pretend the bad guys were coming." His fingers formed guns as he faced the door. "I'd have everything ready. They wouldn't stand a chance against me."

Just like Grayson to see the possibilities instead of the obstacles. At four years old—soon to be five—he had the sweetest optimism about life. Rachel would like to take a scoop of it with her wherever she went. She ran a hand through his soft hair. "Totally, buddy. You'd have the fastest guns, for sure."

Grayson walked the open stretch of floor, boots echoing against the wood. He stopped at the end of the room, head tilted in concentration. "Think Dad would let me move out here?"

She managed to stem the laughter bubbling in her throat. "I don't know about that, Gray."

Though she could understand his interest. The place did have a certain charm—if she looked past the mess that had been left behind. For a family, it would be tiny. But for one or two people? Cozy. Quiet.

If she could get this place cleaned up, maybe *she* could move out here for the next month or two. She could give Olivia, Cash and the boys their house back while still being around to help and spend time with them. Rachel pressed the pause button on her rampant thoughts. The idea was crazy. The house might not be falling to pieces, but it would take too long if she attempted it on her own. Rachel could admit it was as tempting to her as Grayson's fort was to him, though.

"Auntie Rachel, can I go outside?" Grayson had already zipped through the small bathroom and bedroom and must have gotten bored with the space.

Liv let Grayson play outdoors by himself for little bits of time, so Rachel thought the same rule could apply here. "If you stay within five steps of the house."

"Five giant steps?"

With his little legs? "Deal."

"Front and back?"

"Just front. That way I can keep an eye on you through the windows."

His nose wrinkled as if to say he didn't need that kind of supervision, but then he scampered outside.

She moved into the bedroom, watching through the old, white-wood-framed glass window as Grayson scooted down the porch steps, and then, true to form, counted out five long strides from the house. When he reached the limit, he bent down, grabbed a stick and began drawing in the dirt.

Rachel wandered to the east bedroom window and scanned the horizon. No more sign of the rider who had been there minutes before.

If it had been Hunter, he was gone now. Relief rushed in, cool and sweet.

Sometimes she looked back on what had happened with Hunter and wondered how it had all gone so wrong. How they'd switched from best friends to not speaking at all.

Most people didn't know that Hunter had gotten it into his head to propose to her back then. She hadn't even told her brother, simply because Rachel had known it couldn't happen. Getting married at such a young age might have worked out for Hunter. He'd known what he wanted and that it was here. He was a rancher. It had always been this town, this life, for him.

But Cash had given up a lot for her, and she'd been working on maturing at the time. That hadn't included eloping and throwing away a volleyball scholarship. Even for Hunter.

To say the least, he hadn't understood.

Their relationship—even their friendship—had been crushed.

Something skittered across the wood floor and Rachel screamed. An old brown chair had been left behind in the corner of the room, and she ran for it, jumping up. It wobbled under her weight but thankfully held. Screeches continued to slip out of her as the mouse paused to stare her down, then ran for the edge of the room.

She shivered as it disappeared beneath some warped

trim. *Eek*, that thing had freaked her out. Her heart stampeded, and she sucked in a calming breath, thankful no one was around to see her silly antics over such a tiny creature.

"What are you doing?" Hunter leaned against the bedroom doorframe, arms crossed. Looking casual. Amused.

Her eyes momentarily closed. So it had been him she'd seen. He must have left his hat somewhere, because his hair looked as though a hand had scrubbed through the short, dark blond locks only seconds before.

Stinky, stink, stink. How long had he been standing there? She looked down at the chair under her boots, then back to him, contemplating asking, *God, why? Why Hunter? Why now?*

"Nothing."

"Just standing on a chair in the corner of a deserted house?"

"Yep." Rachel didn't have to explain anything to Hunter. For all he knew, she'd been looking at something on the ceiling. Or examining a crack in the wall. Or checking out her ability to fly if she jumped from the chair.

The real question was, what was he doing here?

He motioned to the floor. "Tell me that wasn't a reaction to the cute baby mouse that just went through here."

Rats. He'd witnessed her dramatics.

"What happened to the country girl I knew? The one who could ride as fast as the boys. Wasn't afraid of snakes. Got dirtier faster than anyone else."

"Most of that was true, but I faked the part about snakes. I was afraid of them. Just didn't want to admit it. If I had, you would have tormented me with them."

He laughed, the lines on his face softening. "Well played." He nodded toward her strange standing place. "Don't suppose you want any help getting out of here." His dimples flashed. "You know, so that mean, scary mouse doesn't get you."

"I'm fine." The mouse was long gone. Wasn't it? Either way, Rachel wasn't going to do anything to prolong being in Hunter's presence. Even if that creature came back out. Ran across her boot. Gave her the heebie-jeebies again.

She could handle a little rodent. Just not the man looking at her with far too much amusement.

Besides, with all of the noise they were making, the mouse would be miles away.

Rachel only wished Hunter would follow suit.

"Don't you have a ranch to run?" Rachel huffed loudly enough to blow the walls of the house down like the big bad wolf in the three little pigs story.

Hunter tried to stem the curve of his mouth, but it wasn't working. He'd forgotten how much fun it was to rile up Rachel. "Trying to get rid of me?"

Her head tilted, ponytail bouncing with the movement. "Am I that obvious? Because I'm trying to be."

Despite claiming she didn't want help, she was still standing on the chair. He might be enjoying her predicament and annoyance with him just a bit too much. It had been a few years since he'd gotten any emotional response from her, and he kind of liked knowing he still affected her, even if it meant she wanted to smack him.

"All right, princess." The name earned a scowl as he approached her chair/throne and offered her a hand. "Let's get you out of here."

Her body language screamed *get lost* and *don't touch* in one easy-to-read display. "What are you doing?"

"Helping you."

"I told you, I'm fine." She made a shooing motion. "Just go."

"Now, Rach. I'm not so much of a jerk that I'm going to let you get mauled by a mouse." Her squeak of indignation and the fire in her eyes told him how she felt about that comment. "Come on." He grew serious and dropped the teasing act, re-offering his hand. "Let's go."

"No, thank you."

He'd also forgotten just how stubborn she was. When they'd been younger and first started hanging out, it had taken Hunter some time to prove she could trust him. Rachel'd been the queen of building walls and defending them. Eventually he'd gotten through. And once he had, it had been worth it.

But she'd had years to rebuild. Which meant they could be here all day. And, honestly, he just didn't have time for that. Despite what she thought of him, he'd heard her scream when the mouse had spooked her, and he wasn't going to just leave her stranded.

Before he could analyze how mad she'd be, Hunter bent and scooped her over his right shoulder.

She screeched and whacked him on the back, where the upper half of her body hung. Wiggled trying to break free. He strode through the bedroom and living room, one arm looped around her legs so she didn't fall to the floor with all of her squirming.

"What are you doing? Put me down, you big ogre."

His chest shook with quiet laughter as he exited through the front door. Rachel's nephew Grayson played nearby, destroying an anthill with a stick. He only glanced up for a second—not the least bit concerned about the racket his aunt was making or the fact that she was slung over Hunter's shoulder—and quickly went back to his digging and investigating.

Hunter deposited Rachel on the front porch. "This far enough or do you need me to go farther?" He adopted a serious face and nodded toward the field. "But who knows what-all is out there. Could be a spider or, even worse, a crow—they make scary noises. I've heard stories about them swooping down and snatching up small children. You're a skinny thing. Can't be too careful."

This time her hit landed on his arm. He chuckled, which, judging by the way her face had turned as menacing as a thunderstorm, was only making her more upset.

"Are you done making fun of me yet? I don't appreciate you taking the liberty to cart me around like a sack of feed." She growled the last bit, crossing her arms over a simple white T-shirt that made renewed laughter catch in his throat. He'd been too amused and distracted by her antics inside to notice what she was wearing. Most often when she came home to visit and he caught a glimpse of her, she was dressed up for church. Always looking so put together. Usually in heels, too. Not cowboy boots and faded jeans and a fitted white T-shirt. The simple outfit almost knocked him over.

Though, right now he'd better concentrate on her not kicking him in the shin. She looked mad enough.

"I think I'm done, though I reserve the right to make fun of you about this again in the future. What are you two doing out here, anyway?"

He'd been out checking for signs of coyotes when he'd spotted Rachel and her nephew. He'd stopped to talk to her because he thought they needed to get some things worked out. Like, was she still planning to help the youth build the float? If not, he'd need to find someone else. Hunter was happy to help with the float building, but he didn't feel qualified to be the only one in charge of a group of teens.

"Grayson wanted to explore." Rachel stared straight forward after answering him, her jaw set in that stubborn look she did so well.

"Did you back out of helping with the youth?"

Her cheeks pinkened, highlighting her freckles. "No. I didn't."

"So you're committing?"

Her gaze snapped to him. Oops. Bad choice of words. When she finally nodded, his worry decreased. "That's good. They need someone like you in their lives."

At that, her demeanor softened a bit. "Did you back out?"

"Nope. Wouldn't want you to lose out on the delight of working with me."

That earned him an eye roll and a shaking head. Just like the old Rachel.

He nodded over to Grayson, who was now inspecting under the front porch as though he might find a treasure. "Ran into Grayson on my way in and he told me he was planning to move out here."

Cute kid. Always dressed like a miniature cowboy, that one. Boots. Jeans. T-shirt. Coupled with scrawny arms, a mop of brown hair and eyes that brimmed with curiosity.

"I wish."

"What's that mean?"

Rachel peered through the front window before releasing an audible sigh. "Cash's house is so crowded with me added in. Grayson was asking if this could be his fort, and I was thinking the same thing. That I want to move out here."

"With the mouse?"

Was that a halfway smile claiming her mouth? Hunter should call the *Fredericksburg Standard*. News like that could make the front page.

A visible shudder followed. "Definitely not with the mouse."

"You know, you can get rid of mice. The place didn't look too bad when I was in there. Seemed mostly cosmetic. Cleaning. Paint. Looked like someone had the law on their tail and left half their belongings. Granted, you were screaming like someone was after you, so I didn't get a great look."

"I could never do it on my own, and I'm not asking Cash. He has enough to do."

"I would help you." The words were out of his mouth before he had time to think, but once they registered, he decided the idea wasn't so crazy. If he was going to follow through with the two of them getting along and putting the past behind them, he might as well jump in with both feet.

Curiosity and concern mingled in the depths of her distractingly beautiful green eyes. Maybe even a bit of fear. "Why?"

"Why not?"

It was easier to answer that way than to tell her the truth. *I don't want to turn into my father* seemed like a strange answer. There was one thing he'd never seen his dad and mom do—make amends. Forgive. Move on. Therefore, that's exactly what Hunter planned to accomplish.

And this way, when Rachel did her next disappearing act for the job she wanted and came back to visit her family, she and Hunter would be able to get along. Wish each other well.

She studied the toes of her camel-colored boots as though they held the answer to all of the world's problems. "It was nice of you to offer, but I can't accept."

Couldn't? Or wouldn't? He could pretty easily guess the answer to that. Her response didn't surprise him. She wasn't the type to welcome his offer—or anyone's for that matter—with open arms. Nope. Rachel had always had a bit of an edge to her, and that was putting it nicely. The woman had more spunk in her pinkie finger than most people had in their whole body. It had been one of the things he'd liked about her back then. Still did.

"We need to get back." Rachel shut the front door of the house. She grabbed the small cowboy hat propped on the stair railing and tromped down the steps, heading for their horse and calling Grayson at the same time.

After a few seconds of complaining from the boy, Rachel and Grayson mounted up. They took off with quick waves in his direction.

She was sure in an all-fired hurry to get out of here. Away from him. Not that he blamed her. He'd been a jerk when they were younger. He'd asked her to stay when he shouldn't have.

Some people just weren't built for this life.

Hunter had learned that lesson too well. A painful brand had been burned into him because of his mother's unhappiness. She'd detested ranching and small-town living. Yet Dad had convinced her it would grow on her one day. He'd pursued her until she'd agreed to marry him and live on the ranch. Hunter had heard the beginning of their story many times.

But the middle and end had never improved. In all of his childhood memories, his mom had been sad. Lethargic. Broken. When he was nine, she'd given up pretending and left them. Moved to Dallas.

After, Dad had sunk further and further out of reach. It wasn't that they didn't see each other. It was that they didn't really talk about anything besides ranchTing. His sister, Autumn, had been his saving grace. Three years older, she'd taken to mothering him.

Hunter wouldn't copy his father's mistakes again. He'd been selfish asking Rachel to stay and marry him. She'd only been eighteen. He'd been twenty. Hunter had watched his mom live a life she didn't want. He'd witnessed her unhappiness. He'd known better than to ask Rachel to do the same, yet he'd been grasping at straws to keep her in his life.

And, in the process, he'd lost her completely.

Suggesting they get married had been impetuous of him, and when Rachel had said she loved him but she couldn't, he'd reacted so badly. Out of hurt, he'd pushed her away.

Not a shining moment for him.

But it was time to turn all of that around. Hunter had been at a loss about how to prove to Rachel that they could get along again. She'd built so many walls between them over time—and he'd only been too happy to help her hold them steady—that he wasn't sure where to begin.

But now that he knew about the house, she'd given him the perfect way to start.

He only hoped it wouldn't backfire on him.

Chapter Three

Rachel surveyed the small ranch house from the door-way, frustration zinging along her spine. It was Wednes-day, and she and Grayson had gone out for another ride. He'd been antsy after it rained all day Tuesday, and he'd wanted to visit the house again—which he'd started re-ferring to as his fort. But since they'd been out on Mon-day, someone had been here. Supplies were sitting just inside the door, paint cans included. The mountain of trash was gone.

All fingers pointed to Hunter, since no one else even knew what she'd been thinking. What part of *no* didn't he understand? She did not appreciate his intruding in her life like this.

Rachel slipped her cell phone from her pocket, hoped the reception would work and called her friend Val. The two of them had been best friends since junior high, and the fact that Val still lived in Fredericksburg was, for Rachel, a definite plus in being home. They'd kept up their friendship over the years—one of the only peo-ple Rachel could claim that about. Val had always been levelheaded back when Rachel had been anything but.

Now she hoped the two of them were on a more similar plane. Except, at the moment, *level* was not a feeling Rachel was experiencing.

"Hey," Val's voice sounded in her ear. "Connor is eating mac and cheese, which means I'll probably have to go in a sec when he puts a piece of it up his nose even though I've tried to teach him not to do that a million times."

"Okay." Not for the first time, Rachel thought what a strange thing motherhood was. "You are never going to believe what Hunter did."

"Ooh, what?"

She explained about finding the deserted old ranch house, running into Hunter and the conversation that had ensued. "And now he's started fixing it up after I told him no. I didn't even know he'd been out here and a bunch of stuff got done."

"Huh." Prolonged silence came from Val's side of the conversation. "That's...horrible?"

"It is horrible! I don't want him involved in my life."

"Technically he's not involved. You weren't even there when he did anything."

"Whose side are you on, anyway?"

A stifled cough-laugh combination answered her. "I mean, how could he just help you like that when you didn't even give him permission?"

"Your sarcasm is impressive."

"Thank you. I learned it from you. So, do you want my old-married-lady advice?"

"You've been married two years, so I don't think that qualifies you as headed out for pasture yet, but sure." Rachel's mouth curved despite her annoyance with Hunter. "Hit me with it."

"Let him help. You're out of space at the house. I'd offer to let you stay here—"

"You guys don't have room for me, either."

"That's why I'm telling you to accept his offer. At some point, you need to let go of what happened between the two of you. This is the perfect opportunity."

"No."

"Just...no? That's all you've got?"

"Yep." Rachel might be using toddler logic right now, but she didn't care to adjust her maturity level. She didn't have to explain her feelings, did she? How could she, when she didn't even understand them herself? "Why would he do this?"

"Maybe he likes you." Val stretched out the phrase, sounding as though she was imitating one of the second-grade students she taught.

"Ha." Rachel swallowed, mouth suddenly devoid of moisture. "That's not funny."

Laughter floated into her ear, then stopped abruptly. "Oh, no." Resignation laced Val's tone. "There went the mac and cheese. Gotta go."

They disconnected and Rachel glanced at the pile of supplies. What was Hunter thinking? Could Val's joking insinuation be true? Was Hunter trying to...? No way. He couldn't have feelings for her. Could he? He had talked to her more in the last few days than he had in years. *Was* he trying to rekindle things? It made no sense, especially since he always seemed annoyed or offended by her presence. At least, he had before this visit home.

Rachel didn't know what to think. It couldn't be. But why else would he do something like this?

It wasn't like he hadn't gotten a crazy idea regarding them before. His suggestion they get married had been completely unexpected.

Back in high school, Rachel had made some stupid decisions about guys. She'd dated one she would rather forget and had done a number of things she regretted during her teenage years.

In the last part of her senior year of school, when she and Hunter had first started hanging out, she'd been wary of making another mistake. Another stupid decision about another guy. But she'd quickly noticed the differences in Hunter. He'd been genuine. Always respectful. He'd made her laugh. He was one of the few people she'd talked to about her parents and he'd talked to her about his mom.

They'd hung out a long time before they'd even so much as held hands. Their first kiss had been…heart pounding. They'd been on a walk. He'd been teasing her about something, and the next thing she knew, he'd stopped, buried his hands in her hair and kissed her. Kissed her as though she was oxygen and he needed to breathe. After, he'd backed away. His grin slow. Easy. "I knew it." Then he'd grabbed her hand and kept walking while she stumbled to find coherent thought again.

She'd fallen for him. Hard.

Falling for him had been the easy part. But even back then, they'd known she was moving for school. The knowledge had hung over them like a storm cloud that followed their every step. At first it hadn't been menacing—just something to deal with in the future. But as the time for her to leave had neared, the cloud had changed from might-rain-sometime into a dark, severe-weather thunderstorm.

They'd avoided talking much about her looming departure for college, neither of them knowing what to do about it.

The week before she'd been set to move, they'd been sitting on the porch swing at his dad's house, concern over the future stealing their words, when Hunter had squeezed her hand. "Don't go," he'd said. Her head had snapped in his direction. "Stay. I know people will say we're young, but I don't want to do life without you. Marry me." At first, his eyes had flashed with surprise at his words, but then he'd leaned toward her as if the idea had gained momentum. "We should get married. We could elope."

Rachel remembered precisely how she'd felt. Like a car had rammed into her. She'd loved Hunter, but had known instantly that she couldn't. As much as the thought of leaving him had hurt and refusing him had felt like the hardest thing she'd ever do, she'd been certain she had to follow through with her plans.

Her stomach had tied itself into thousands of knots. She'd tried to tell him how much she cared about him... but that she couldn't stay. Couldn't marry him. Not at eighteen.

In the middle of her explanation, he'd shut down. His eyes had hardened. And then he'd told her to go. That if she didn't feel the same way about him as he did about her, she might as well leave immediately. In the next week, before she'd left, they hadn't even seen each other. It had been so painful.

She couldn't do that again. Rachel didn't know what Hunter was thinking, but she had to talk to him. They were going to be working together with the youth. They'd be seeing enough of each other that she had to make sure she was clear with him about her future plans and that nothing could happen between them. They couldn't go back down the road they'd once traveled.

It was Wednesday. Tonight was the first night of working on the float with the teens. She'd head over early and have a conversation with him.

She had to. Because, despite having moved on from their younger years, she knew she couldn't survive that experience twice.

"Are you sure you know what you're doing?"

Autumn was perched on the desk in the barn office/storage area while Hunter rummaged through the bins the church had given him for float decorating.

When he glanced up, her pointed look told him she expected an answer. His sister packed a lot of punch for five foot two. But despite her petite size, she'd always played and fought just as hard as the boys.

"Yes, I know what I'm doing." He set aside two bins. "Just because you're older than me doesn't mean you're wiser."

"You are correct." She twisted her light-brown hair over one shoulder. "Age doesn't matter, but I am wiser."

He didn't bother answering that sassy comment.

"You do remember what happened the last time? I mean, I think Rachel's great and all, but you were a mess when she left."

He didn't need the reminder. "I wasn't a mess." He might have been a small version of that word. "But that's not going to happen again. This is about being a friend. What I should have been to her in the first place before I let stupidity cloud my judgment. She needed someone to be there for her, and back then I made it about me and what I wanted. She deserves to be treated well, and while I didn't accomplish that the last time, I am going to this time."

"So, you're just going to help her with this house whether she wants it or not?"

"Pretty much."

"And you're trying to prove…"

"That I'm not Dad." The words slipped out, and Hunter almost rolled his eyes. How did Autumn always pull information out of him he didn't plan to give?

Her eyebrows stitched together. "Hunter, you're nothing like Dad. You work hard, so I guess you have that in common, but that's about it."

Except for the part where he'd asked Rachel to stay and he shouldn't have. And the next part, where he'd been a jerk and reacted badly when she'd said no. Autumn didn't understand because she and her husband Calvin had met when they were older. Dating…marriage…it had all just fallen into place for them without any stupid decisions to atone for.

"Think about it this way. If you knew you couldn't have Calvin as anything more than a friend, wouldn't you want that? And if you'd hurt him, wouldn't you want to rectify that?"

Autumn studied him. Finally, she nodded, but her brow remained pinched. "I just don't want to see you get hurt."

He tapped a fist on his chest. "I'm practically a superhero with all of these muscles."

She groaned in response, then stood and rubbed a hand over her growing belly. His nephew was coming in about three months, and Hunter was more than ready. It had been a rough pregnancy, and Autumn had been sick for much of it.

She might be his older sister, but he still felt protective of her. Which meant he understood her concern about him. But she was just going to have to trust him. Hunter had prayed over this decision, and he felt peace about it. Moving on and regaining a friendship with Rachel was the right thing to do.

Autumn stretched her arms over her head, accompanying that with a huge yawn. "I'm hungry."

"What's new? It's been an hour since you last ate."

"Jerk." Humor puckered the skin around her eyes. "I'll see you later."

She let herself out through the office door, and a few seconds later he heard her car start. Hunter grabbed the extralarge gray tote filled with float-building supplies and strode toward the open end of the barn where the flatbed trailer waited.

Rachel stood just inside the large sliding doors. She looked fighting mad. Gorgeous—no surprise there— but not happy. He changed course, walking in her direction.

Was she just here early for the first night with the youth? Or had she found out he'd been at the house? Based on her expression, he'd say the latter. Hunter had hoped helping make the place livable for her would work in his favor, but he was starting to doubt his plan.

Rachel wore a green sleeveless shirt with pressed flowered shorts. Coupled with sandals that daintily looped around her ankles, she looked perfectly put together, yet she still had that edge. The one that said, *I don't belong in this Podunk town. I'm meant for more and don't you forget it.*

Though he read her message loud and clear, it didn't stop him from appreciating the sight. He'd thought jeans, a T-shirt and boots might do him in the other day, but as it turned out, it didn't matter what she wore.

Caused a bit of trouble, that. He wasn't supposed to be noticing how she looked—though, really, it would be impossible for him not to. He was supposed to be renewing their friendship. And he wasn't off to a great start by the look of it.

He set the large tote on the ground by their feet. "Hey, you're here early."

"I need to talk to you before the kids arrive."

"About the float?" He could only hope.

"No."

Ah. So she'd found the stuff.

"I assume it was you who started working on the house?"

He didn't have anything to hide. "I did."

"I wasn't even serious about it. It was just a passing thought. Why would you do something like that?" Her breath hissed out. "It doesn't even make sense. I'm only going to be here for a month or two."

"What's Cash planning to do with the house?"

"I don't know. I asked Olivia what happened with it. She said the last renter trashed it, and Cash hasn't had time to deal with it since."

"So after you live there for the summer, he can rent it out again. If none of his ranch hands want to lease it, one of ours might. We're not talking about remodeling the place. Just cleaning it up and making it livable so you can stay there while you're home."

Silence reigned. Rachel opened her mouth, then closed it. Finally, she lifted one freckled shoulder. "I guess that makes sense." Just that movement made his mouth go dry. Pesky attraction. At least he'd had a lot of practice shoving it down and ignoring it over the years.

"But why are you helping me?" Her forehead crinkled. "Why would you do that? I don't know if you've forgotten, but you and I aren't on the best of terms. It makes no sense. Unless…" She might as well spit it out since he didn't have any idea what she was trying to say. "Hunter…" Her voice lowered as though someone was hiding around the corner and might overhear them. "You're not trying to restart anything between us, are you?"

What? She thought he was…oh, man. He hadn't even considered that working on the house would make it look like he wanted something more with Rachel. Partly because the idea hadn't even crossed his mind. But, of course, she couldn't read his thoughts.

"We can't." Her lips pressed together. "I can't."

He agreed with her. He couldn't, either. "I'm not trying to start anything between us. I was just sick of—" he raised his hands "—fighting. Not being able to be around each other. Figured it was time to move on. I knew you could use a hand, and this is what friends do."

"So you're not…"

"Nope."

"Oh, good." Distress dropped from her frame, her sigh audible. And a little bit offensive. Did she have to be *so* relieved about it?

Whatever. It didn't matter. Hunter wasn't on the hunt for a wife, anyway. What had happened with his mom and then Rachel had tainted that idea for him. He just wanted a quiet life on the ranch. No drama. No women who didn't want to be there. If he found someone, that would be great, but he wasn't going to do backflips to make it happen. He could be content on his own.

"I'm not trying to pursue anything more than friendship with you, so you can relax. I wouldn't do that to you." Or to himself. "I would never ask you to stay again, Rach. I know you don't belong here." Silence swirled between them, the past rearing up with ugly memories. "Promise. You can trust me."

Her pained glance told him she wasn't so sure about that.

"Will it put you at ease if I'm not the only one working on the house? Because Brennon called and said he and Val want to pitch in. They're planning to come out Saturday."

"What?" Exasperation laced the word. "When did you talk to them?"

"Just a bit ago. Why?"

Sounded like she muttered *traitor.* "What is up with all of you? I didn't even ask for help. This is crazy."

"Are you really surprised? Don't you remember what it's like living in a small town? This is how it is. When someone needs something, everyone pitches in. That's the deal. You'll just have to adjust to the idea."

"And what if I don't want to?"

Hunter knew the answer to this question. His life had taught him this truth numerous times. "You can't always get what you want."

Chapter Four

Somewhere along the way, her plan had backfired. Go over there and tell Hunter to back off. Rachel pictured herself doing that "go to the mattresses" punching move like Meg Ryan in *You've Got Mail*, fists jabbing into thin air. And then failing miserably—also just like the character in the movie.

Of course she wasn't going to let her friends work on the house without pulling her own weight, which meant she'd be spending even more time with Hunter. Rachel had definitely lost the battle to avoid him while home. He'd said he didn't want anything more than friendship with her—and she believed him—but she still didn't relish being in his presence. Even the friendship he wanted felt too far out of reach for them. Their bridge had washed out years before, and it was too late to rebuild.

Get used to having people intrude in your life, he'd told her.

Well, she didn't plan to. Rachel wasn't about to let her guard down and have him and a whole town rushing in.

Was. Not.

Liv had agreed that Rachel staying at the house was a great idea. Which meant now she just needed to broach the subject with her brother.

They'd just finished dinner, and Grayson had run off to play.

Olivia collected Ryder from his high chair. "I'm going to change his diaper." She shot Rachel a look, as if to say, *do it, already*, then headed up the stairs.

Fine. "Cash, what are you planning to do with the little ranch house?"

Her brother finished a long swig of milk. "Not sure. T.J. took off about three months ago. He quit without notice and made a mess of the place. I haven't had the time or energy to deal with it." His back pressed into his chair. "I might just let it sit there. Not a real fan of being a landlord, anyway."

"What if someone got it back in functioning order for you? And then lived there for a little bit and then you could rent it out again?"

His forehead creased. And why wouldn't it? She was talking in circles.

"I want to live there while I'm home. It will give you guys your house back—"

"This is your house, too, you know."

"Technically it's yours." When they'd settled things with their parents' will, Cash had bought out her portion of the house. She hadn't wanted it.

"This will always be your home. You are always welcome."

The strangest prick of emotion touched her eyes. "Okay." She heard him. But no matter how many times he said it, she would always feel like a leaf scraping along the pavement in a gust of wind. Rachel didn't really belong anywhere.

When she moved to Houston, maybe she'd settle in. Put down roots.

"If I can stay at the house, I'll be close by. My friends are going to help me get it cleaned up and functioning, and then when I leave, you can rent it out again. If you want to. Hunter even mentioned that one of his ranch hands might want to rent it if you'd rather not deal with knowing the tenant personally."

"I don't know." Cash pushed his plate forward and propped his arms on the table. "I just don't know how safe that would be for you."

She laughed.

He scowled.

"Oh, you were serious? I thought you were kidding around, because it's in the middle of two ranches where I know both families. The only visitors would be crickets and frogs." And hopefully not mice.

Her brother did remember she'd been living on her own for the last six years, right? In a city much bigger than this one. A bit of that old friction radiated between them. Rachel had been excellent at pushing Cash's buttons in high school. Admittedly, she'd enjoyed every minute far more than she should have. But she really didn't want to fight with him now. She wasn't that girl anymore. Or, at least, she made a serious effort not to be.

Liv came back downstairs with Ryder on her hip and paused at the edge of the table, glancing between Cash and Rachel. "It's weird how Rachel rarely comes home to visit. Here she has all of this tension waiting right here for her and she doesn't even take advantage."

Rachel couldn't help it. She laughed, earning another frown from her brother.

Ryder bounced in Olivia's arms and Rachel reached for him. He came right to her, and she lifted him in the air, earning a flash of baby teeth, a sloppy grin and a bit of drool. When she settled him on her lap, he grabbed the R pendant she wore on a simple gold necklace and gave it a firm tug. Thankfully the chain withstood his efforts.

Grayson might be her favorite nephew for adventuring, but Ryder was the best at snuggles. His hair was a few shades lighter than Gray's. Almost had an auburn shade to it. No one knew where that had come from. His cheeks were squishable, and the boy was as solid as a summer day was long. Liv talked about percentiles and other momish mumbo-jumbo, but Rachel just knew her nephew was built like a one-year-old linebacker.

Oliva dropped into the chair next to Cash. "Rachel and I talked about the house earlier today, and I think it's not such a crazy idea. In fact, I think it's a good one. How many times have we said we need to get it cleaned up, even if we don't decide to rent it out again? You don't have the time. Rachel and her friends will have it done in a few days. We could even use it as a guesthouse if you don't want to rent it. My parents could stay there when they visit. And Rachel would have a place to crash when she comes back to see us."

Every time Rachel thought she couldn't love Olivia more, she was proven wrong.

"Rachel staying there makes perfect sense," Liv continued. "I'm surprised we didn't think of it earlier."

Cash looked part contemplative, part concerned. "I don't know why she'd want to live in that hunk of a house, anyway. It's as big as a cracker. And old." And Rachel didn't know why her brother was talking about her as if she wasn't in the room.

"And quiet. And quaint." Liv sat up straighter in her chair. "Maybe I want to move out there."

"Ha." Cash's eyes narrowed. "Not funny."

She stacked their empty dinner dishes. "Who says I'm joking?"

A shaking head–grin combination came from Cash. "You'd miss me, city girl."

Before Liv could retort—and Rachel had the utmost confidence her sister-in-law would have had a good one—Cash turned serious again. "I don't know that it's a good idea for you to be out there by yourself, Rach. Something could happen."

"And now this sounds like when Rachel was in high school." Liv jumped in, compassion evident despite the disagreement. "She's twenty-four. Not seventeen. Besides that, by the end of the summer she'll likely be living in Houston by herself." If anyone could talk her stubborn brother into something, it would be Liv. "Ryder cries at night, and even though he's going back to sleep, he's waking up Grayson who's crawling into bed with us. I, for one, am exhausted. I'd like to sleep without a foot in my mouth." Olivia scooted closer to Cash, placed her elbows on the table and propped her head in her hands. "Do you see this face? This is a tired face."

In answer, Cash leaned forward and pressed a kiss to her lips. "It's a beautiful face."

"Flattery will get you everywhere."

While Rachel appreciated Liv having her back, she wasn't sure how much PDA she could handle. The house might not be worth it. "I like to think I've evolved into a mature version of myself, but you two are kind of grossing me out right now. Somehow you are just as annoyingly sappy as you were when you first got married."

They laughed.

Rachel glanced at the time on her cell, which was lying on the table. She'd told Hunter she would meet him at the house tonight so they could start working, assuming her brother wouldn't have any issue with it. She should have known better. The two of them had always been like rams, crashing into the other until one of them won. Though they had gotten better over the years since she'd been gone. Rachel appreciated her brother far more now than she had when she'd been a teen. She'd pushed and clawed at him in high school, but he'd never backed away from her. Even at her snarky teenage best.

She could do the house without his agreement; she knew that. He'd come around eventually. But it wasn't about permission. It was about getting along. She liked the idea a whole lot better without her brother being upset. They'd been down that road one too many times before, and she had no desire to repeat history.

Which was why, if he really didn't want her to live in the little house, she wouldn't.

"Well?" The toe of Rachel's flip-flop tapped under the table, her gaze steady on Cash. "What are you thinking?"

His hands rubbed his eyes as he leaned back in the chair. "Are you actually waiting to hear my opinion?"

Ryder shifted on Rachel's lap, as though he wanted to get down. "I'm a docile version of my old self. Sweet. Compliant."

Cash snorted as she deposited Ryder on the floor,

and he toddled toward the couches and toy bin. He'd only recently started walking, and every few steps he'd tumble to the floor and crawl a little before pulling himself back up on a piece of furniture.

An accusing look flashed from Cash to Rachel and Liv, though it was tempered with amusement. "If I even attempt to say no, the two of you will conspire and do it, anyway."

Liv's hand landed on her sternum. "Rachel and me, scheme? That would never happen." She shot a grin in Rachel's direction. "Plus, you heard Rach. She's the picture of innocence these days."

In the past, her name and *scheme* in the same sentence would have offended her, even though it likely would have been true. But now Rachel could embrace the humor instead of the embarrassment.

"I'd never forgive myself if something happened to you," Cash continued. "I know you can make your own decisions and take care of yourself. It's just having you here makes me think you're my responsibility again."

"We've been over this." He'd struggled so much with protecting her after their parents passed away. Over feeling responsible for things that weren't in his control. "God's got me covered. I've always been in His hands." And it was true. Rachel didn't always understand the way God answered prayers, but she did know what-ifs got a person nowhere. "Something could just as easily happen to me in Houston as it could here. There are no guarantees."

"Well, that's not helping anything." A reluctant tilt claimed one side of his mouth. "At least promise me you're going to fix the broken latch and put the best lock known to man on there. In fact, I'll get the replacement lock. I'll spring for whatever supplies are needed to get it functioning again. Only makes sense if we're going to benefit from your work."

She whooped and ran over, hugging him.

"Who did you say was going to help you?"

The feeling of excitement plummeted as she straightened. "Val and Brennon on Saturday, and…Hunter."

"He's a good kid."

The *kid* part made her mouth lift. Hunter was eight years younger than Cash.

Her brother's head cocked to the side. "Didn't the two of you—"

"Yep. We did. But that was then. Nothing to do with now."

Cash raised palms in defense. "Okay. Just…be careful." He began to drone on about safety with power tools and being sure to ask Hunter about the sink, because it was leaking. And how they should wear masks when they painted. But Rachel was already light-years ahead of him.

They might have slightly different takes on his warning, but Cash didn't have to tell her to be careful twice. Because that's exactly what she planned to do.

Hunter left the door of the house open while he worked. The summer heat clung to him, and the light breeze brought in much-needed relief. He swiped the back of his arm across his forehead. Sweat changed places and he winced. Good thing he wasn't trying to impress Rachel this time around. He was pretty sure he looked a mess. He'd come straight from the ranch, only stopping to nuke two of those sorry excuses for frozen burritos for dinner. He'd wolfed them down in his truck on the drive over, then wished he'd have made three.

He heard Rachel's vehicle approach and turn off. A few seconds later, her footsteps sounded on the porch.

"Hey." She paused inside the doorframe as though waiting for an invitation to come in.

"Hey."

Hunter grabbed the water he'd brought along from the counter and took a long swig while Rachel stepped inside.

She wore a yellow T-shirt, cut off jean shorts and flip-flops. Her toenails were painted with bright blue polish, the color of one of those slushy drinks kids loved.

She walked over to the bedroom and peered in before facing him.

"You got a lot done."

"Mostly just removed all the trash. It's not so bad without the junk."

"Sorry I'm late. Cash threw a hissy fit about me living out here alone. Like I'm not old enough to take care of myself or something."

Eye roll. Hair toss. Hunter bit down on his amusement since Rachel wouldn't take kindly to it. He might doubt his fair share of things, but he was certain of that.

"You're fine. I just got here. Did you work it out?"

She'd bent down and started looking through the paint cans he'd brought over. "Yep. Where'd you get all of this paint? I should pay you for this. Cash said he'd cover supplies since he's the one benefiting. Said to tell you thanks for helping out." She paused. Let out an audible breath. "And that anyone who puts up with me should get a medal for it."

Quiet laughter shook his chest. "He did not say that."

She met his eyes, a smile tracing her lips. "He was joking. He did say thank-you, though."

Hunter nodded toward the supplies. "There's no need to pay for any of that. I had some stuff left over from my house. Didn't buy a thing."

"Your house?" Her tone carried surprise.

"Yeah, I built a few years back."

"Don't you live with your dad?"

"Nope. My house is on the west side of our property. Not too far from here." Hunter knelt to look through the tool bag he'd brought. "You know my dad. He had his fists wound so tight he would never have let me have any ownership of the ranch until he left this earth. I threatened to work somewhere else if he didn't let me buy in. I wouldn't have, but he didn't call my bluff."

Rachel's mouth swung open as if on a hinge. What had she thought? That he'd just sat around pining for her all of these years? Hunter grabbed an adjustable wrench, dropped to the floor and scooted the upper half of his body under the sink, wincing at his thoughts. Those old hurts always seemed to pop up with her when he least expected it. Friendship didn't hold grudges.

"Cash said that's leaking." Her voice sounded hollow from his perch inside the cabinet.

"I can tell. That's what I'm working on."

"Oh. Okay." He heard Rachel shuffling things around while he tightened the retention nut on the supply valve. After she'd left for Colorado, he'd gone through varying stages. Hope that she'd change her mind. The knowledge that she shouldn't. Moping. He'd been great at that. And then anger. He'd stayed there for a good long while. At himself. At her.

Now that he was working on letting those responses go, the load on his back was starting to feel a bit lighter.

Starting.

Not that he expected her to let him in easily. He hoped by the time they got this house back to rights, he and Rachel would have a functioning friendship again. Maybe even a bit of trust. Or, at least, he would have gotten past one of her walls. Hunter didn't want to spend the rest of the time she was home dealing with her still halfway despising him.

"How's your sister?"

Hunter loosened the water line then scooted out from under the sink to grab the joint compound. "Bossy. She still does the books for the ranch, and she's about to have a boy. Kinsley's beside herself to have a little brother."

"Tell her congratulations from me."

"I will." He went back under the sink to apply the compound. He wasn't sure exactly what was causing the leak, but hopefully if he hit most of the reasons it could be happening, he'd get it stopped.

Once he'd finished, he wrenched himself out of the cabinet. Not so roomy in there. Rachel had started sweeping the floor, and now she was going at cobwebs that hung from the ceiling with the broom. One must have dropped on her, because she released the broom and started swiping her arm as if whatever had landed there might do her in.

He stifled a laugh. She'd definitely gone city over the last few years.

Her phone dinged as Hunter pushed up from the floor, body aching from being in the cramped space. When had he gotten old?

Rachel's fingers flew over the keys as she answered whoever it was. She might not have a ring on her finger, but that didn't mean she wasn't attached to someone. He swallowed the heat that rose at the thought. Nothing for him to get upset about. Though he was curious.

"Boyfriend?"

She jumped and fumbled the phone, dropping it, then catching it again before it hit the floor. Slid it into her back pocket. "No boyfriend."

Hunter pulled out one of the kitchen drawers and placed it on the countertop. He grabbed his drill from the tool bag. "Did I ruin it for you for life?"

His teasing earned a forced smile. Didn't look like she was ready to call him her best friend just yet. "No. I just didn't really have time to date in college. I was too focused on school. Unlike high school, where I focused on the opposite."

He tightened the screws holding the drawer together and the *zzzz-zzzz* of the drill filled in the silence.

"You weren't so bad in high school."

She snorted in answer then swept the mess she'd collected into the dust pan and deposited it in the black garbage bag he was using.

Sure, Rachel had made some interesting choices before they'd dated. Had a boyfriend Hunter would have liked to punch in the jaw. But she'd come around. Hunter had known she would. By the time they'd started hanging out, she'd already begun changing. Didn't she know that? Still, the years had made a difference. On Wednesday, she'd been amazing with the kids.

"You were great with the teens last night." He slid the drawer back in and started on the next.

"Thanks. I feel like I barely got to know anyone."

The night had gone quickly. Mostly spent dealing with suggestions for the float. After a bit of fighting among the kids, Rachel had suggested they draw their ideas and put them up for a vote at church this Sunday. A good way to make peace. The teens had spent the rest of the night brainstorming in groups, so Rachel hadn't had much opportunity to talk with them yet. Hunter knew a few from church, but some were new to him, too.

"It will come with time." Not that she had a lot of that.

"I guess."

"So, if by some strange chance you don't get this job in Houston, what's your plan?"

"There's a teen rehab program that my friend works at in Dallas. I'll apply there if this doesn't pan out. It sounds like they're looking to hire." She didn't have to fill in the rest. Hunter could read between the lines. Her options were anywhere but here.

There wasn't even a minute chance of her staying. That was good for him to know and remember. Rachel had a *Do Not Touch* sign flashing on her forehead, and Hunter planned to obey the directive this time around. Besides, after one night of seeing her with the teens, he could tell the job she wanted was exactly what she was meant to do.

Hunter faced the countertop again and replaced the drawer. "You seem…content with the career you've chosen. It fits you. You did the right thing leaving when you did."

He felt her gaze heat the back of his neck and turned. Her jaw had slacked. She blinked once. Twice. "Leaving you or this town?"

Emotion rushed across his skin. "Both." If she hadn't gone, she wouldn't have this new opportunity that was obviously right for her. She'd be stuck. Unhappy, just like his mom.

"Going to school was the right choice. It would never have worked between us." He couldn't believe he'd just said those words out loud. What was he doing, bringing this up? But she should know the truth. "You wouldn't be able to do what you do with the kids if you hadn't. After one night, I can tell you were made for it."

It almost looked as though a sheen of moisture had glazed her eyes. "Thanks." She opened her mouth as if to say more, and then her demeanor changed as fast as a flash of lightning. She shuttered, attention dropping to the floor. "I should start on the bedroom." She snapped up the broom like it was her saving grace and took off as though another mouse was on her heels.

That was odd. What just happened? Hunter had thought they were actually getting somewhere by talking openly. But, then again, he was dealing with Rachel. What had he expected? The woman warmed at the slowest possible pace. She'd stopped letting him in emotionally a long time ago. One confession, one moment of baring his soul regarding what he should have told her years before wasn't going to instantly mend what had happened between them.

Twenty might not do the trick, either.

Chapter Five

The metal bed frame pressed into Hunter's palms as he stood just inside the door to Rachel's new hideaway on Saturday morning. "The room ready for me to set up the bed?"

"Yep." Rachel paused from wiping down the kitchen cabinets. "The paint is probably still a little damp, so maybe set it up in the middle of the room and I'll just slide it over later when the wall is dry."

"Sounds good. Smells like a pool in here." One Hunter wouldn't mind taking a dip in.

"Bleach." She tossed the rag into the bucket by her feet. After rolling her neck, she swiped the back of her arm across her forehead. "It's hotter than a june bug in July."

His cheeks creased at her declaration and returning accent. About time her southern roots showed up. "Did Olivia take off?"

They'd had a slew of helpers show up. Cash last evening. Olivia this morning to help paint, but she'd had the boys with her, so she'd spent most of the time corralling Ryder. And Val and Brennon had been working most of the day, painting, cleaning, moving stuff in. They'd cut the workload in half and had been a Godsend. Currently they were out grabbing the last load of Rachel's stuff from Cash's barn where she'd been storing it.

"Yeah. She wanted to get the boys down for naps since we're heading over to Lucy and Graham's for dinner." Rachel cracked open a bottle of spring water and took a long drink.

"Nice."

She smiled, head shaking. "Chaotic."

"Lot of kids between the two families."

"Five. Though Mattie is like an adult."

True. Any time Hunter saw Graham and Lucy's oldest at church, she was never loud or crazy. She always had a shy smile, but she observed more than she destroyed.

Rachel turned back to her cleaning, and Hunter accepted his dismissal without complaint. He'd gotten used to Rachel's behavior on Thursday and Friday evening while they'd worked on the house, and then again today. The second she realized she was opening up to him—like even that simple conversation right there—she shut down and poured herself back into a task. Hunter felt like a kid on a teeter-totter, but he wasn't sure how to get off the equipment and find any stationary ground with Rachel.

Moving into the bedroom, he began piecing together the simple bed frame he was letting Rachel borrow along with the mattress set. It had been sitting in his guest bedroom, unused, since he'd replaced his a year ago.

Once Hunter finished, he strode back into the kitchen. No Rachel.

He found her standing on the front porch, fanning herself with a small towel. He stepped around to face her.

"What's up?"

"Val texted that they were on the way, so I was checking for them. And trying to cool off. Why did I think moving back to Texas was a good idea?"

"Just think about the winter. You'll love it."

Her eyes narrowed. "You might be right."

With Rachel, that much of an admission was a victory. "I got the bed frame set up. I need to carry the box spring and mattress in. Want to help me?"

"Sure. You got the frame set up that fast?"

"Yep. It's just a simple metal frame. No fancy headboard or anything. Hope it's up to your citified standards—"

"One of these days you really need to learn when to stop talking."

Hiding a grin, Hunter took off for his truck. People might call him crazy, but this was the Rachel he preferred. Because when she was sassy and sarcastic with him, he knew he was getting the real deal. And he liked that truthful version.

When he reached the truck's tailgate, he glanced back to see Rachel had followed him.

"I'll pull and you catch the other end when it slides off." He lugged the box spring halfway off the truck bed, then slowly slid it the final few feet while she grabbed hold. She must have lost her grip, because the other end crashed to the ground, a puff of dirt rising up.

"Oh, no!" She slapped a hand over her mouth. "Thought

I had it. Sorry! Ah, man. Now it's all dirty. You let me use it and I'm already ruining your stuff."

She thought he'd be upset about a little dust? Did she not remember what he might be covered in at the end of the day? "It's fine. No problem." He motioned with his head toward the box spring. "Though I'm still holding this if you hadn't noticed."

Rachel tugged on her ear, adopted a casual stance and made no move to help him. "Did you say something? Sounded like a fly was buzzing around my head."

Mouth quirking, he scooted the box spring up until it stood tall and rested against the tailgate. "I'll have Brennon help me when they get back. Wasn't sure what I was thinking, asking you to haul it in, anyway. You're only half as big as a minute."

She squeaked with indignation. "I'm a mammoth."

"You?" A laugh burst out of him. "Are you joking?" Rachel might be tall—around five feet ten inches—but nothing else about her even remotely represented that word. "You're not embarrassed about your height, are you?" He didn't remember any conversations about that in the past.

"No. At least I can use it to intimidate people." Her chin jutted to the side with playfulness.

"You don't intimidate me one bit." An internal buzzer sounded, calling Hunter's bluff, and it had nothing to do with height. Because underneath all of Rachel's bravado, she was sweet and smart and funny. And gorgeous. What guy wouldn't get a little tongue-tied around her? She even smelled good despite the oppressive heat—something girly and tempting that he couldn't name.

Although he believed he was doing the right thing, moving on from the past and mending things with Rachel, he still doubted at times. Some moments, it was downright painful to be around her. When he caught glimpses of her sassy side. That smile. The way she teased him. Those reminders of what they'd once had were hard to stomach. But he knew better than to gallop down a treacherous hill. They were friends, and friends was all they'd be.

If she even let him have that.

Rachel's arm had a smudge of white paint on it, and Hunter reached out without thinking, sliding his thumb along her skin. He'd thought the paint would be wet and wipe off, but it had already dried. And then, like an idiot, he didn't let go. Suddenly he was twenty again, driving in his truck with his girl, a hand on her arm, the warm sun—

"What are you doing?" Rachel snapped her arm against her chest as though he'd scalded her. If he had to pick a word to describe the way her eyes flashed, he'd settle on *displeasure*.

"I just…you had some paint there."

Brennon's truck rumbled down the drive.

"Oh." Her look changed to curiosity, as if to say, *Why did you touch me*? *Touching is off-limits.* He wanted to answer her silent query with *I don't know* and *I agree*.

Brennon backed his truck up to the house while Rachel gave a forced, tight-lipped smile. "One last load and we'll be done."

The doors on the truck opened and closed. She backed a step in that direction, then paused. Held his gaze. "Hunter, thank you for your help on the house."

No edge remained. Only softness. Sincerity. "I couldn't have done it without you."

She took off to catch up with Val and Brennon, leaving Hunter reeling. The woman switched from teasing to upset to earnest in a matter of minutes. This was exactly how she'd messed with him in the past. She built walls to keep everyone out—she even had with him, at first. But when she let them down—when her sweet, sincere side showed like just now—it could take a man's legs straight out from under him.

He'd done this for the right reasons, hadn't he? It wasn't about restarting anything with Rachel, was it?

No. It couldn't be. He was at the point where he really did want to regain their friendship—no ulterior motives.

It was just...being with her reminded him of all the reasons he'd liked her in the first place, and that was trouble.

Their futures were headed in different directions. Staying wasn't an option Rachel was considering—she even had a second job opportunity lined up—and his life was here. He owned part of a ranch. He couldn't walk away from that. Plus, he didn't want to. Hunter loved his work.

So he needed to remember why he'd started all of this and stick to that plan. No veering off course.

He had a feeling the safety of his heart depended on it.

"Okay, kids. It's time to let Auntie Rachel go free." Lucy Redmond, Olivia's sister, approached the couch where her daughter Lola and Rachel's nephews had fake tied Rachel up.

Lucy had moved to Texas years ago. She'd met and married Graham Redmond, a local doctor, and adopted his daughter, Mattie. Since then, the two of them had added two little girls to the mix. Graham was very much outnumbered, though he didn't seem bothered by the abundance of females in his house.

Dinner had ended a while ago, and since then, a game of cops and robbers—with a cowboy flair—had been in full swing. Two-year-old Lola was dressed in a princess costume. She'd spent the evening running around the house, Ryder toddling after her, while Grayson "saved" her from Rachel, who'd agreed to be the robber.

Rachel had pretended to have her hands tied together when she actually had three-month-old baby Senna—Lucy and Graham's newest addition—sleeping in her arms. The soft, sweet bundle had done the same for much of the evening despite the decibels of noise surrounding them. Occasionally she yawned in a perfect little O.

"Wait!" Grayson approached, hands on his hips. "The prisoner has to eat a worm to gain her freedom."

Rachel's nose wrinkled. She assumed the request was fake, but with Grayson's infatuation with all things slimy, slithery and of the insect family, she didn't know for sure.

She tossed her hair back dramatically as best as she could with her hands occupied. "I refuse to eat your detestable worm. I'd rather spend the rest of my life in captivity."

The haughtiness in her voice caused Lola to go into a fit of giggles, but Grayson kept a straight face, as though truly contemplating her refusal.

His small chest deflated. "Okay, I'll let you go this time, but next time…" His head shook. Rachel somehow resisted a smile. He was so stinking cute she wanted to eat him up. But she definitely had no plans to eat a worm, no matter how much she adored her nephew.

Lucy transferred Senna from Rachel's arms to her own. With her free hand, she directed the children until they stood in front of Cash and Graham, who were still sitting at the dinner table talking. "You guys should ask your dads to take you outside." The enthusiasm in Lucy's voice transferred to the kids, and they were soon jumping in front of their dads, their requests loud.

The two men shared an amused look but stood without argument, as if knowing their fates were sealed.

"All cowboy cops and damsels in distress to the backyard." At Graham's call, Grayson and Lola raced for the back door. Ryder followed but fell behind, so Cash scooped him up on his way outside, giving him a lift.

Once the whole lot of them had exited out the back door, a strange silence descended on the house.

Being at Lucy and Graham's was a bit like being smack-dab in the middle of a circus, but it was a homey sort of chaos.

These were Rachel's people. Olivia and Lucy had adopted her too, in a way. Starting back when Cash first met Liv. And then Rachel had gotten to know Lucy well when the two of them had both lived in Colorado. Now, they included her in anything sisterly.

Nights like this tugged on Rachel's heartstrings a bit too much. Maybe Lucy was right. It was time to stop being an auntie. Time to go. Rachel was afraid if she did too many more of these dinners, they'd begin to chip away at her resolve not to live in this town.

"I should probably get going."

Lucy propped her one free hand on her hip. "Oh, no, you don't. We haven't even had a chance to catch up. You've been too busy wrangling children all night."

Olivia had been wiping the kitchen countertops but now came over and sat next to Rachel on the couch. Lucy placed Senna in a brightly colored infant seat and buckled her in. Her eyes opened. She observed her surroundings, but didn't make a peep. Weren't babies usually more demanding? Connor had been so fussy that Val hadn't sat down for months after his birth.

Lucy popped the pacifier into Senna's mouth and then dramatically dropped into the chair across from them. The back of her hand landed on her forehead. "Raising children is not for the faint of heart."

Rachel's mouth curved. "Speaking of kids, where is Mattie tonight?"

"She's at a friend's house. She already had plans, so we didn't want to make her cancel. So…" Lucy's eyebrows waggled, face alight. "Tell me everything. How's it going? Liv says Hunter's been so helpful with the little ranch house."

Funny that Lucy didn't mention anyone else who'd pitched in. And so it began. "He has been. We just finished up today." Rachel couldn't help tacking on a clarification to address Lucy's insinuation. "And he's just being neighborly."

"Neighborly." Loose blond curls cascaded over the other woman's shoulder as her head tilted. "Is that the new name for it?" Despite the teasing, Rachel couldn't find it in herself to get upset. Lucy managed to do pretty much everything in life without offending. Most everyone who knew her instantly loved her.

Though Rachel should still set things straight. "Honestly, there really isn't anything between us. We're just attempting to get along at this point."

And they were doing okay.

Now that they were done with the house, Rachel could relax. Take a full, deep breath again without the masculine smell and presence of Hunter interrupting her every thought.

Somehow, she'd survived working with him unscathed.

The man had a way of sneaking past her defenses, but she'd managed to spend countless hours with him in the last three days and not...what? Get hurt? Let him in too much?

All of the above.

"Hunter and I are just friends." Sort of friends.

Lucy's nose wrinkled. "But that's so boring. He's adorable."

"I'm right here!" Graham's voice carried from the kitchen into the living room. "I had to grab some bottles of water. Do I need to stay and police the rest of this conversation?"

"Hollywood, you know you're the only one for me."

Graham chuckled, looking equal parts besotted, amused and mistrusting. "Don't let her push you, Rachel. She always has something up her sleeve."

"What?" Lucy let out a squeak, fingertips landing against the neck of her casual electric-blue cotton sundress. "I would never." She grinned at Rachel and Olivia as the back door shut and Graham returned to the kids. "I have always liked Hunter. He was one of the first people I met in town." She toyed with her outrageously gorgeous wedding ring. "I found out later that it drove Graham crazy, even though Hunter was too young for me. And of course I fell for the first guy I beaned in the head when I moved here."

Olivia and Rachel laughed. Only Lucy.

"Seriously, though," Lucy continued. "You don't feel a thing for Hunter?"

Rachel shook her head.

"Not even an iota?"

"Nope." Her conscience screamed *liar*, but she ignored it.

Her feelings for Hunter had been buried years ago. Except for that moment today when he'd touched her arm. Every nerve in her body had sprung to life. She'd immediately shoved down her reaction, hoping Hunter wouldn't notice. Her response to his touch had only made her more determined to stay at least one foot away from Hunter at all times. Maybe two. How was it she could know he wasn't right for her and be attracted to him at the same time? His looks were easy to swallow, like the first sip of hot coffee on a frigid morning. And those dimples—they were overkill. Shouldn't God have spread out some of that attractiveness instead of depositing it all in one man?

On top of that, Hunter walked through life with a laid-back vibe that instantly put people at ease. To Rachel, that only made him more troublesome.

The whole time they'd been working together, she'd had to remind herself to focus on the house. Keep her head down and do the work. Not let Hunter get past her

defenses. Her thoughts had sounded like Olivia back in
the days she'd coached Rachel in volleyball. *Do this!
Don't do that! You can do it!*

If only her heart took direction so easily. It had always had a soft spot for Hunter. Foolish organ. It needed
to remember she was moving. That she wasn't ready for
anything more than a surface-level friendship with him.

"Well, boohoo." Lucy's disappointment only lasted
for a few seconds before she perked up. "So, any chance
you want me to set you up while you're in town? I'm a
great matchmaker."

"She's a horrible matchmaker," Olivia chimed in,
humor lacing her voice. "Her record is zero for three."
She patted Rachel's capri-clad leg. "Not that I don't
want you to find someone who would tempt you to
stay, Rach. Of course I do. But I also understand the
need to make your own life. Sometimes starting over
means finding home."

If Rachel had learned anything while being stuck in
this town, she'd confirmed that she really, really loved
her sister-in-law.

Olivia asked Lucy about her plans at the dance school
she owned and somehow managed to run along with
mothering three children, and Lucy filled them in on
who she'd found to help out with the kids once classes
started back up in September.

Minutes later, their chat was interrupted by screams
coming from the back door. Cash held Ryder, whose
cheeks were dripping with plump tears, while the rest
of the group tromped in behind him. "Injury. Nothing
serious. Just bonked his head and needs his mama."
Cash deposited Ryder into Olivia's outstretched arms.
"I think he's tired."

"I'm sure you're right." Olivia swept a hand over Ryder's forehead, and his cries turned to whimpers. "We should go."

Despite complaints from the kids following that comment, the next few minutes were spent rounding up toys and getting everyone out the door.

Rachel followed Cash and Olivia home in her Jeep—they'd driven separately since she'd been late getting over to Lucy and Graham's. When she reached the turn for the house, she waved and split off while they kept going.

She pulled up to her new place and got out, quiet greeting her. Contentment zipped along her spine at the knowledge that Cash and Liv had their house back and she had this little haven.

Her furnishing were sparse since she'd sold a lot before leaving Colorado. Besides the bed from Hunter, she had a comfortable chair and side table in the living room. A small kitchen table and two chairs, plus a dresser she'd found for ten dollars at a garage sale in town. Cash had donated an old microwave he'd had stored out in the barn. For how long she planned to stay, she didn't need anything more.

Rachel popped up the steps, stopping on the porch when a strange humming noise disrupted the otherwise peaceful night. She walked back down and around the side of the house to find the source.

Her feet froze a few yards from her east window, where an air-conditioning unit now perched. She knew it hadn't been there before, because she'd wondered more than once while they were working on the house how she was going to sleep in the stifling summer heat.

Cash had been with her tonight, so he couldn't have

installed it. And Val and Brennon didn't have any extra money to be throwing at this hunk-of-junk house.

That left Hunter.

Pushing himself into her life. Without permission. Again. She was never going to forgive him. She stomped up the front steps, marched inside and slammed the door behind her. Her head fell back as ice-cold air washed over her.

Okay, maybe she could be persuaded to extend some grace.

Rachel changed into pajamas and made the bed, then propped her pillows against the wall, grabbed her cell and climbed in. Peace. Quiet. And air-conditioning.

Hunter was wearing her down. "What am I supposed to do with him in my life again?"

The empty house didn't answer her. But the southern politeness ingrained in Rachel dictated that she thank him. She swiped her phone screen, and then her fingers flew across the keys. Thank you for the air-conditioning. It's amazing.

She had almost given up on hearing back from him when her phone notified her of a text.

What's this about an air conditioner?

I know it was you. Don't even try to pretend.

That knowledge sank into her bones. No one noticed her quite like Hunter did. At that scary thought, she texted him again.

Just accept my gratitude. Once he did, she could put the phone down and move away from how he made her feel.

His text came back quickly.

Actually, your brother got the air conditioner. He asked me to install it as a surprise for you.

Cash. She glanced at the time. He'd be getting the boys into bed, then crashing himself. Rachel would thank him in the morning. It was sweet of him. She should have known he wouldn't be able to *not* take care of her while she was home. But instead of making her irritable, like it would have when she was younger, she was thankful. She really did have the best brother in the world—it had just taken her a few years to realize it.

And Hunter... Her pulse galloped. He'd spent his Saturday night installing an air conditioner in this old house simply because her brother had asked him for a favor. It sounded exactly like something Hunter would do.

Earlier, when she and Hunter had been talking about her going to dinner at Lucy and Graham's, Rachel had thought about asking him if he wanted to come. But something had held her back—fear, she supposed. If he was really a friend, she would have invited him, knowing full well Lucy would welcome another person. Especially Hunter. Rachel should have included him. But, instead, she'd taken the opportunity to put more space between them. And what had he done? Something for her.

She'd been keeping him at arm's length so that he couldn't worm back into her life. But who was she kidding? He'd already made his way in. She was simply denying it. Punishing him. Holding on to all of that old hurt.

She texted him.

You still want to be friends, huh? Even after spending the last few days with me? I would have thought you'd be running by now.

A small part of Rachel had assumed if she held out, Hunter would give up. Go away. Leave her alone. But he hadn't. Just like the last go-round, when he'd pursued her despite her initial attempts to resist him.

Nah. I still want to bless you with the precious gift of my friendship. I can put up with you if I have to.

Humor creased her cheeks.

You mean I can put up with YOU if I have to.

His text dinged back quickly. Who is this again?
She laughed. Hunter got her in ways other people didn't. He knew when to tease her and when to be serious. She liked that about him. She liked him. Spending time with him had reminded her of that fact.
Not that she planned to admit that to him yet.

You're a dork.

I don't accept abusive texts. I think you have the wrong number.

Rachel snuggled lower into the sheets, amusement threading through her.
She couldn't believe how effortlessly he'd eased back

into her life. More than one night over the last six years, she'd lain awake wondering how it had gone so wrong between them, fighting the temptation to call or text him.

But this wasn't about the past. It was a chance for something different for the future.

In the last three days of working together, Hunter had broken down a bit of the barrier that had stood between them. Rachel didn't have a clue how to stop him. Or if she wanted to. She only knew she couldn't let herself go beyond friendship. But maybe, just maybe, she could allow that.

It would be safe, wouldn't it? They both knew everything that stood between them and how much they would lose again if they messed this up. Her fingers hovered over the keys. Had he already moved on from their conversation? She couldn't resist checking.

Go to sleep, Hunter.

I will when you stop texting me.

Her laugh echoed off the walls that were void of decoration, reminding her just how little time she planned to spend here. But she'd deal with that thought another day. Because, at the moment, she felt content. Almost peaceful.

Ever since she'd started college, she'd been driven. Like she had something to prove. Busy chasing the next goal. But tonight she could sleep soundly without her future to-do list tightening like a vice around her chest. And while she might pretend it had nothing to do with the man on the other end of the phone, once again she'd be lying to herself.

Rachel turned her phone on silent, clicked off the lamp and burrowed beneath the blankets. If she fell asleep with a smile on her face, no one needed to know about it.

Chapter Six

"I still can't believe the church chose this design for the float." Rachel held up the paper that boasted a sketch of a goalpost with a large sign hanging from it that read *All things through Him*. Someone had drawn football players in uniform and a gaggle of cheerleaders littered across the float, faux green grass beneath their feet.

Hunter had bent to look through one of the bins next to the flatbed trailer, and she had to nudge him with her knee to get his attention. "Hello?" She shook the paper near his head.

"Huh?" He looked up. "Oh." A half grin made his dimples sprout. "It's Texas. Have you forgotten that football is almost a religion here?"

"No, I haven't." Her nose wrinkled. "But it's a football float, not a church float."

"Of course it's a church float." He pointed to the drawing. "Right here along the skirt at the bottom, the church's name is big and bold."

She laughed. Resisted slapping a hand against her forehead. "Okay, I get the concept of everything, even sports, as honoring to God. After all, volleyball made a huge impact on me. If I hadn't met Olivia when I did…" She shrugged.

Hunter had gone back to sorting supplies, but Rachel was having a hard time letting go of the float concept. "It doesn't have anything to do with the Fourth of July." Though there were a number of flags and hand-made red, white and blue decorations drawn in along the sides. "Did you see the other sketches on Sunday?"

No answer. Hunter just kept digging in the bin for something. Rachel felt pesky—like the moths that would descend on Colorado in the summer, invading every nook and cranny and driving everyone crazy.

Just when she was starting to doubt he'd even heard her, he glanced up and answered. "Yeah, I did."

"So you know there was one that actually had an Independence Day theme? With an immigrant family arriving in the United States. And the Statue of Liberty. And a small church replica with a Welcome sign hung across the door."

"I saw the same thing as you."

"That should be the float we build."

"I agree." Hunter shot her a pointed look. "But *someone* told the kids that whichever float got the most votes at church would be the winner. No arguing."

A sigh escaped. "I did say that, didn't I?"

"Yep. You're kind of bossy, in case you didn't know it."

"That's because I know more than you when it comes to dealing with teenagers. If the kids hadn't agreed to that, they'd be fighting about it right now."

"Like you are?" He stood. "Aaand, good to know you're humble."

Laughter bubbled from her throat. Strangely enough,

being teased by Hunter felt good. Only it didn't last. His smile fell quickly, much like it had been doing since she arrived. Her counselor instinct told her something was off, but she couldn't put her finger on what.

Hunter nodded toward the growing group of kids. "We should probably get started."

"Okay." Rachel wasn't used to an all-business Hunter. Was he upset about something? Did it have to do with her? He'd fought for a friendship between them, but now she couldn't help wondering if he regretted that.

He walked toward the kids and she followed. There were more teens than last week. A good thing, since they had a lot to do. Maybe Hunter just wanted to get things rolling. She could understand that.

"Hey, guys, listen up." Conversations slowly trickled to a stop, and the teens faced them. "We're going to form teams to work on different sections of the float." Hunter pointed to the right side of the group. "The netting to go under the trailer…" Then he pointed to the middle. "The goalposts and grass…" Finally, he motioned to the left. "And red, white and blue decorations and flags. Rachel found directions online for most everything and they're posted by each station. Some things we'll have to improvise, so let us know if you have questions."

Most of the kids split off. Hunter called out to two girls standing a few yards away who were talking and hadn't moved toward a project yet. They glanced in his direction, looking as though walking over to Hunter— and Rachel, since she was right next to him—equaled cleaning up manure. After a moment's hesitation, the girls approached.

"This is Rachel Maddox." Hunter motioned to her,

then to each girl. "Bree." Strawberry blonde, Rachel noted, committing her name to memory. "And Hannah." Dark hair. Equally pretty. Rachel didn't remember seeing either of them the week before.

"I've known these two since they were up to here." His hand sank to around hip level. "Bree's dad and I were in a men's Bible study together."

Bree folded her arms, stance somewhere between wary and downright irritated, and Rachel recognized a bit of herself from high school. She pressed her lips together to keep from smiling at the girl's obvious annoyance.

"So, what part of the float are you girls thinking about doing?"

"We're going to work on the red, white and blue decorations." Bree raised one perfectly manicured eyebrow toward her expertly highlighted hairline. She probably meant to come off strong and aloof, but the hurt radiating from her overpowered her attempt. Rachel tucked away that knowledge to dissect later. Bree's partner in crime had remained quiet, but both sported looks that shouted *bored. Old people alert.*

Had Rachel really acted this way when she was younger? Sigh. Double sigh. She'd *so* been these girls. And she'd had the same snarky attitude toward Olivia when she'd first moved to Texas.

Rachel would have to apologize to her—again— when she saw her tomorrow.

She asked a few questions in an attempt to get to know them. Hannah answered, but Bree only gave stilted responses. After the third one-syllable reply from Bree, Rachel gave up.

"It was nice to meet you girls." They took her comment as the dismissal they'd been waiting for, turned in unison and bent their heads together as they crossed the barn.

"They were…sweet." Actually, Hannah had been fine. Just on the quiet side.

Hunter watched their departure, concern pulling on his mouth. "Bree's parents are getting divorced, and she's been a mess lately. I'm sorry for her rudeness."

Now the hurt/brave act made sense. "I'm not offended. I was her in high school."

His warm caramel-brown eyes crinkled at the corners. "You were never that bad."

Rachel simply raised an eyebrow in response, then laughed when she realized she'd just imitated Bree's facial expression. But Hunter didn't join in her amusement or say anything further. His gaze had already drifted over her shoulder, unfocused, lost in some thought she wasn't privy to. Something was going on with him, but flipping through options of what it could be wasn't getting her anywhere.

"I'll go check on the guys doing the goalposts." Hunter nodded toward the group. "They look confused."

"Okay, I'll just—"

He was already gone, long strides taking him across the barn. He wore a heather-brown T-shirt tonight, the fabric worn yet still intact. Jeans that looked as though they'd lightened with washing and sun and time. Boots, of course. It was like a uniform with him, and she didn't have any complaints. It fit his normally casual, laid-back vibe, which had been squashed by something tonight.

"Check on these kids." Rachel spoke to herself and wandered over to a group, only realizing at the last minute it was where Bree and Hannah had migrated to. Oy. Well, she knew how to speak teenager, didn't she?

"Do you guys have any questions?"

Bree barely glanced in her direction. "Nope." The word crackled with tension. "We've got it."

Rachel decided not to push. To give the girl some space. She backed up a step. "I'll be over here if you need anything." Good thing the school she wanted to work at couldn't see her now. Leadership skills with teens? Absolutely none. Ability to communicate with students? Nope.

The kids would accept her eventually, she assumed. Once they warmed up to her. And that's about when she would be leaving.

"Hey, Rachel, how's it going?"

At the sound of a woman's voice, she turned. Hunter's sister, Autumn, approached, wearing jeans, cowboy boots and a yellow V-neck maternity T-shirt that had ample room for her round tummy. Her light-brown hair was twisted into a no-nonsense braid.

"It's going." Rachel waved a hand in the direction of the kids closest to her. "They love me, obviously." She added some Bree sass to her voice, and Autumn's face wreathed with humor.

"They'll come around."

"That's what I'm hoping." She asked Autumn about her pregnancy and her daughter Kinsley, then finally voiced the question weighing on her mind. "Is Hunter... okay? He's not acting like himself today."

"You noticed that, did you?"

Rachel nodded.

Autumn seemed to contemplate her words, studying her brother across the space with a pinched brow.

"This was the week our mom left."

The quiet words detonated like a bomb, and Rachel's throat constricted.

"He always gets this way. Quiet. Not himself. Hunkers down for the week, and then he comes back. I guess I'd be more concerned if he didn't turn into himself again after, but he always does. I've tried to help him process before, but nothing I do makes any difference. I just have to let him work through it."

"I'm sorry." Rachel hated this for them. "Are you okay?" It wasn't just Hunter whose mom had scrammed. Rachel's stomach twisted at what they'd both been through.

"No." A sad smile accompanied the answer. "Yes and no." Her hand etched over her pregnant belly. "I just can't imagine leaving them. Being a mom makes it seem all the more impossible."

"You guys ever hear from her anymore?"

"Sometimes. But it's few and far between. She sends birthday cards some years. Very occasionally there's a phone call." She gave a disgruntled laugh. "I'm actually amazed she remembers the dates."

A rendition of "My Girl" blared to life, and Autumn snagged her phone from her back pocket, glancing at the screen. "I need to take this. I was going to ask Hunter something but I'll just do it later." She swiped to answer and waved goodbye to Rachel as she walked toward the barn doors.

Rachel scanned the room, finding Hunter still stationed across the barn. He was working on the goalposts with a small group, but he didn't seem to be conversing much. Definitely not joking around like he normally would. It physically pained her to think of how much he'd been hurt when his mother left. She wanted to hunt the woman down and confront her.

Rachel might not be able to do that, but she could be there for Hunter. He'd been good to her. A true friend.

Now it was time for her to do the same thing for him.

On Thursday evening, Hunter wrenched off his boots in the mudroom located at the front of his house, tossing them with more force than necessary toward the spot they usually sat.

He headed straight for the shower, intent on washing off the long day. It was almost eight o'clock, and he hadn't eaten dinner. A recipe for disaster with him. Not that he'd needed anything to push him into a bad mood. He'd handled that all by himself, and he'd been nursing it all week.

When he'd popped into the main house to grab something for lunch today, Autumn had called him crabtastic. But her bark was way worse than her bite. She was just concerned about him. He'd told her he was fine, but his sister had a habit of not listening to anything he said.

After showering, he threw on a clean pair of jeans, fresh socks and a green T-shirt emblazoned with the name of Kinsley's preschool—Kid Kapers—along with the name of the orphanage they'd sold the T-shirts to help support. Which explained why Hunter had another two just like it in his drawer. He'd just walked into the kitchen, planning to scrounge for some dinner, when someone knocked.

Autumn. She seriously could not leave well enough alone. What did he have to do to convince her that, yes, he was okay, and no, he did not need a pint of ice cream and a chick flick to make him feel better? That was Autumn's comfort cure, not his.

He twisted the knob and wrenched the door open. "Autumn, you're driving me—"

Rachel stood on the landing, wearing a simple white top, a casual navy skirt that landed above the knee and yellow sandals. "Crazy?"

"I was going to say nuts. But that works."

"Siblings will do that to you." No explanation followed for why she was at his house, but something brewed in her striking green eyes.

Did he even want to know? "Come in." Maybe he could eat while she spilled whatever was on her mind.

She didn't budge. "Actually, I need you to put your shoes on."

His head cocked to the side. "Something wrong?"

"No."

He stood stock-still. Somehow he was missing something.

"What's going on?"

"I need you to put your boots on." She stretched out every word as though talking to a mischievous two-year-old. What in the world? The temper that rarely ignited in him turned up a notch.

"Listen, Rach, I'm not sure—"

She grabbed his arm and yanked him over to the mudroom bench, then shoved him down. The combination of surprise and curiosity took the fight out of him, and he sank to the seat. She pointed to his clean boots, and after one long breath, he obliged.

Women. Would he ever understand them?

"Did my sister send you over here?" He slid on one then the other, adjusting his jeans over the tops.

"No." She tugged him off the bench, then out the front door. "Your sister has no idea I'm here." After shutting the door behind them, she paused. "Do we need to lock it?"

"Nah."

Rachel still had hold of his hand, sending an electrical current up his arm. She pulled him across the gravel drive to where her Jeep was parked.

"Is this the same Jeep you had in high school?"

"Yep." She opened the passenger door and motioned for him to get in. "Still runs, so no reason to give it up."

She went around to the driver's side as he got in, climbed inside and started it up.

"It smells good." He sniffed toward the backseat. "Like Italian."

"If you're a good boy, you might get some of that."

His stomach rumbled in agreement, and she took off down the drive, the tires kicking up dust. She'd left the top off the Jeep, and the wind toyed with pieces of her hair that had come loose. She paused at the end of the drive to redo it, twisting the light locks into a low bun that whispered against her neck before turning for town.

"Did you cook?"

"Puh-lease. You really think I've changed that much? I can only handle meals with four ingredients or less."

If she wanted to feed him, she could have just dropped off food. Wasn't that what most people did? And why in the world did she want to feed him?

They reached town, and Rachel parked the Jeep near Marktplatz. Hunter could hear the twang of a country band performing, and the memories of the two of them doing this very thing flooded him. Back when they'd dated, they used to park near whoever had live music playing, sometimes grabbing food or ice cream, and listen to the band play in the background while they sat in her Jeep or his truck and talked.

She dug into a bag in the backseat and handed him a Styrofoam to-go box and a set of plastic utensils while the warm summer air surrounded them, heavy with traces of humidity and the simplicity of the past.

"I assume you haven't eaten, or if you have, that you'll eat again."

Both true statements. He wasn't one to turn down food. Especially Italian.

She pulled out the same-sized container for herself. His held lasagna and a piece of warm bread, hers manicotti. The tantalizing scent of baked garlic and cheese made his taste buds kick into high gear. Hunter was so hungry, he didn't even bother asking what was going on. He just dug in. They ate in silence as the day edged into night and music drifted toward them.

Using the last bit of bread to sop up the remaining sauce, Hunter popped the morsel into his mouth. He gave a contented sigh and closed the box. That had almost been worth it. But he'd still rather be home than here.

"You going to tell me what's going on now?" He tossed the container and trash back into the paper bag still in the backseat, then shifted forward again, eyes up and taking in the first twinkling lights appearing against the gray sky.

How many nights had he and Rachel done this very thing? Stared up at the stars and talked. He'd wished on the shooting ones with everything in him.

Those hopes and prayers hadn't come true, though. Rachel tossed her container into the bag, too. It took her a minute to meet his gaze and speak. "Autumn told me this week is the anniversary of your mom leaving. I don't think I ever knew the exact timing of—"

"Her disappearance?"

She nodded.

"Gotta love my sister."

"It wasn't her fault. I couldn't figure out what was wrong with you. You were acting so strange. She was just answering my question."

"Which she didn't have to answer." Wasn't Autumn supposed to be on his side? Hadn't she been worried about Rachel hurting him again? So much for the brother-sister bond.

"True. She didn't. But I'm glad she did." Rachel looked up through the open roof. "You don't have to talk about it. I just didn't want you to be alone with the memories."

He covertly studied her profile while she stared at the sky. This was why he'd missed her. Why he'd been so mad at her for leaving. Rachel had an incredibly soft side that so many people never got to see. Not that she wasn't nice and kind and all of that—she was, whether she thought so or not. But this…this was why it had been so easy to love her.

But his mom's unhappiness and discontentment were the very things that reminded Hunter not to want Rachel to stay when she didn't desire to be here.

"The week before my mom left, she was happy."

Concern wrinkled the skin around Rachel's eyes, the usually bright green fading to evergreen in the darkness. She reached out and squeezed his arm. He knew she was being there for him purely as a friend, but he still gave himself a quick mental warning before continuing.

"It was the most peaceful I'd ever seen her." Unwanted emotion pricked behind his eyes, but Hunter fought against it. Cleared his throat. "She was up early instead of sleeping late, the sadness and dark circles gone from her face. Everything about her was different. Even the way she made eye contact. I remember coming home to find cookies baked one night. I thought..." The disappointment of that week choked him, and he had to swallow before continuing. "I thought she'd finally come around. That she was feeling better, or something good had happened. That she was actually going to be happy with us. I felt so hopeful. I thought my prayers had been answered."

And wasn't that the worst of it? To have faith as a kid and then not have it answered in the way he'd known God could answer? It had taken Hunter years to work through that knowledge. To wrestle with God about it. Eventually they'd tussled to the point where God had won. Hunter trusted Him now, almost *because* of that hurt. He'd had to realize the world was fallen and not what God created it to be. He'd had to trust that what the Bible said was true—that God loved him and had good plans for him. Hunter had chosen faith instead of doubt. But it had taken him a long while to get there.

Rachel had stayed silent. Waiting. Listening.

"Turns out she was at peace because she'd decided to leave. When Dad told me she was taking off...that's when I figured out what had been going on." He'd been nine, but felt as though he'd grown into an adult in that moment. In the realization that she hadn't been getting better. Hadn't wanted to stay for them. She'd been relieved to be running away, even knowing she was going to break her kids' hearts. Or maybe she'd just never really thought beyond her own escape.

Never realized what it would do to them.

Tears were silently slipping down Rachel's cheeks. He wanted to reach over and gently wipe them away but the move would be too intimate. Too much like something he'd once had the right to do. Hunter searched the backseat, grabbed a box of tissues and handed it to her.

She snagged one and swiped under each eye. "You never told me that."

"I put it out of my mind most of the time. But for whatever reason, the week of... It always gets to me. I'm sorry I made you cry." He'd always hated to see her in tears. With Rachel, those occasions were few and far between, but when she did cry, it made his chest feel like it was being run over by a tractor.

"I'm sorry your mom stinks."

His mouth curved. "So eloquent."

"What? It's true." The sound of her laughter reached in, filling the canyon-sized cracks in his heart.

She'd redeemed this no-good day for him. Did she know that? This friendship business was going to be harder than he'd originally thought.

"You were pretty crabby when I forced you out of the house tonight."

He stayed facing her instead of the stars. One view he could have forever. The other would likely only last a few more weeks. "I don't really like you. You totally ruined my night." His grin stretched far too wide to make his words even remotely believable.

She answered his smile with a gorgeous one of her

own. The kind that stole all coherent thought. That had made him suggest they get married even though he'd known better.

"That works out well, then, McDermott, because I don't really like you, either."

Chapter Seven

"I need to leave at five."

Hunter knew his dad had heard him by the way a scowl creased his weathered cheeks.

His father's gray hair was thick under the rim of his hat. The gray had come in slowly over the last decade, reminding Hunter that his dad was getting older. Probably too old to continue ranching for another twenty or thirty years as he'd like to do. Not that Hunter would have a say in any of his father's decisions. Dad had always done things his own way. Rachel might have a touch of stubborn, but his father dug his feet in hard then poured cement around them.

Dad branded while Hunter held the calf's head still and their vet, Willie—who looked about as old as the sun itself—administered shots. Hunter couldn't remember a time when Willie hadn't sported bright white hair. It was as if he'd always existed and never aged. In a simultaneous movement born from years of working together, they let go while one of the hands ushered the next calf down the chute.

"What's that supposed to mean? Think you've got

a nine-to-five job, all of a sudden, and you clock out on Friday?"

A parade of calves had already gone through today, and they weren't done yet. Normally Hunter would never leave something half finished. He worked as long and hard as any of the hands—longer most days. Just like his father. Dad could have quit showing up years ago. Holed up in the office and let everyone else handle the dirty work. But he still worked the ranch every day.

"Nope. I've just got something I need to do."

His dad grunted. "You leave early, we lose money."

So what if they lost a few dollars? Some things in life were more important than making a buck.

It was the youth group lock-in tonight, and Greg had asked Hunter to help. They were going all-out with games and fun activities. Lots of kids were inviting friends, and the RSVP list had grown bigger in the last week, causing Greg to call for reinforcements.

Hunter had been happy to help.

Growing up, his family had always gone to church. Even after Mom left, Dad continued going. But it had felt more like the thing to do and not like a relationship with God. Hunter had learned about God and grace when he'd started attending youth group. That's when he'd grown close to Him. So, was it such a shock he wanted to help provide that opportunity for other kids?

Dad didn't talk about God much, but every so often Hunter would see his Bible out as if he'd been reading it. His father was a confusing man. A mix of hard business and quiet expectations. Hunter had never wanted to let him down or disappoint him. But he'd grown up in the last few years and started standing up for himself. Surprisingly, Dad had given in on Hunter buying into the ranch and building his own place. Maybe because he'd realized he would lose his son if he didn't budge. Hunter would gladly attempt to mend the stilted years between them and move forward like he was doing with Rachel, but he didn't know where to start.

"Yep. You're right. We are spending extra money when I leave." They let the calf go. Waited for the next and repeated the same motions with it. "But I don't want to make the ranch my whole life." *Like you did after Mom left.*

If the words made an impact, his father didn't show it. Hunter motioned for one of the hands to switch places with him and then took off for his truck.

It was a waste to do any more explaining. Dad would never understand. He'd made horrible mistakes with Mom, and Hunter didn't plan to repeat any of them. Especially not with Rachel. They were getting somewhere, and he was feeling freer with each day that passed. The anger and hurt he'd held on to for so many years had been like a weight strapped to his back. But each day, more of that disappeared. He was starting to believe he and Rachel really could move on and have a friendship.

That he might not turn into his father, like he'd feared he would. Dad didn't know how to forgive or let go or move on. He'd let the past turn him gruff and bitter. Hunter was well on his way to avoiding those same blunders.

He'd realized something the other night when Rachel had shown up at his house and forced him out. When she'd saved him from his own sorrows. Or, at least, shared them with him.

She was changing.

Opening up, bit by bit—and not just with him. When

she'd first come home, all the walls had been up and operational. But time seemed to be softening her.

And he was starting to think God might be using him to help with that. This whole journey of letting go and healing what had happened between them might have nothing to do with him. It might have everything to do with her and what God was doing in her life.

And he was okay with that. Willing to be a part in whatever way God wanted him to be. Hunter had given up his own plans years ago. And now he trusted that whatever God had in store would likely surprise him, most often push him and always be better than what he'd expected.

Rachel checked the time on her phone, which was perched on the kitchen table. She and Olivia were having a cup of coffee after dinner at five thirty on a Friday evening—totally something her parents would have done—because she hoped it would help her stay up while wrangling teens at the lock-in tonight. Olivia didn't have the same excuse. Her need for caffeine was based purely on addiction.

Cash was still out working, and the boys were now playing in the living room.

When Pastor Greg had called Rachel yesterday morning, she'd had no idea why his name had popped up on her phone screen. Admittedly her first thought had been panic. Fear that she'd done something wrong with the float or the teens. Visions of high school had flooded back, and it had taken a few seconds of conversation to realize that he wasn't contacting her about a problem—he'd been calling to ask her to help chaperone the lock-in.

That realization had felt like dipping her feet into a pool on an achingly hot summer day. Refreshing to be asked to help instead of being asked to change her behavior.

She'd said yes.

Rachel welcomed another opportunity to show the town she'd changed. That she wasn't the same messed-up kid anymore. She liked people looking up to her. Respecting her. Not headed in her direction to reprimand her for another bad decision.

"Have you heard anything about the job?"

An ache flashed beneath her ribs at Olivia's question.

"Nope." Nothing in the few weeks she'd been home. Rachel had been told it would take time, but she was anxious to find out something. Anything.

"I texted my friend Dana. She works in human resources and she's the one who told me about the job in the first place. She's going to sniff around and see what she can find out."

Rachel was trying to be patient, but it wasn't her strong suit. She'd been stalking the campus online. It was gorgeous, with beautiful old buildings and a grassy outdoor space. She'd be close to the coast. Shops and restaurants at her fingertips. She missed living in the city. Not that this life wasn't good. It just wasn't what she wanted.

But until she heard more, Rachel would just have to keep doing what she was doing. Now that she and Hunter were in a good place and he'd returned to himself after dealing with the emotions of his mom leaving, she could turn her concentration elsewhere.

Which for her, meant Bree. The girl was never far

from her mind, and Rachel assumed God was putting that pressure there for a reason.

She'd heard Bree talking on Wednesday night about going to the lock-in, and it had given Rachel another reason to agree to chaperone. She wanted to get to know Bree better, and tonight would hopefully provide more opportunity to do that.

"I'd better get going. I need to be at the lock-in early for an instructional meeting. I'm sure it takes more than a few rules to keep the kids out of trouble." She shuddered. "Can you imagine what I would have done at something like this?"

Olivia laughed. "You would have caused Cash more than a few gray hairs." She twisted her coffee cup. "But, then again, you know every teenager does stuff—every adult, for that matter, does stuff they regret. That's why there's forgiveness and grace. God doesn't keep a list of mistakes, Rach. And neither does your brother."

She wasn't so sure. Sometimes Rachel felt like people were watching her. Waiting for her to screw up. She'd never been able to shake the thought that her next disgrace was right around the corner. Probably why she worked so hard to make sure that didn't happen.

In school, she'd been so focused on gaining her degrees and succeeding that at times she'd forgotten the social side. Sure, she had friends. But when it came down to it, very few people knew her inside and out.

Olivia did, and her sister-in-law still loved her. That had to count for something.

"You have everything you need for tonight?"

"I packed a small bag and I took a nap earlier. Hopefully it's enough to tide me through."

"They really don't sleep?"

"I don't know. I think they bring sleeping bags. I know there's a girl's quarters and a guy's quarters, and I'm hoping that some of them will want to sleep, which will allow me to do the same."

They both stood, and Olivia gave Rachel a hug. "Don't forget to have some fun."

"I'll do my best." Rachel headed for church. When she arrived, she pulled into the far side of the lot—the portion not covered in jousting stands, a huge blow-up slide, a batting cage and a Velcro wall. A misting tent was set up to help combat the summer heat. The kids would love this. Rachel might even be willing to try something out herself—for the sake of the teens, of course. Just to make sure everything was safe and functioning properly.

She had a bit of a competitive streak in her. Nothing compared to Liv, but perhaps a close second. She'd known there would be games, so she'd worn casual clothes. Capri jeans with a few textured tears and holes, a dark blue V-neck T-shirt and strappy flat sandals that tied around her ankles. She'd thrown her running shoes in her bag just in case she needed them.

She tugged her backpack out of the backseat but left her sleeping bag to retrieve later. Then she strode across the parking lot, not wanting to be late for the meeting in the church library.

When she stepped inside the room, Greg was already attempting to gain the group's attention. Oops. She slid in along the right wall of the filled room and spied a window ledge to perch on in the back. She dropped her backpack on the floor and braced herself on the make-shift seat, stretching her legs out.

The chair in front of her, one of the wheeled seats

that surrounded the huge oblong table in the middle of the room, scooted back until it almost bumped into her sandals. She inched her feet away from its path. No reason to ruin a perfectly gorgeous pair of shoes over someone who obviously lacked personal space boundaries. And...there came that snarky side she tried to tamp down. Rachel glanced up, hoping whoever it was couldn't decipher her true musings, when her mouth filled with dust.

She recognized those shoulders in a charcoal-gray T-shirt, his cropped, disheveled hair and, as he turned slightly to face her, the light layer of scruff covering his cheeks.

Hunter leaned against the back of his chair, stretching its mechanical limits.

"Hey." He grinned at her.

Her traitorous mouth curved in response before she could even decide if she wanted to smile back. The sight of him had her stomach tumbling like a child rolling down a grassy hill. She hadn't known Hunter was helping, hadn't expected to see him. She would have prepared if she'd known. Shored up any off-limits, giddy, girly excitement that might ignite at his presence.

Thoughts about being happy to see him had no business sprouting when she hadn't given them permission.

"I didn't know you were going to be here." She kept her voice to a whisper. "Are you stalking me?"

The faint echo of dimples etched his cheeks before his eyes narrowed. "I didn't know you were helping, either. Maybe you're stalking me."

Greg's instructions continued to drone on: *No boys and girls left together without a chaperone in any part of the church. Roped-off areas are off-limits. Kids found going into them will be sent home without any warning.*

"Don't you have a ranch to run?"

"Yep."

"Don't you have other things you should be doing? How do you have time for this?"

He met her gaze with heat. "I have time for this. It's important."

Sweet man. He certainly had his priorities in order. One day—likely soon—he'd find a woman who wouldn't let him get away like she had. Hunter would be a great husband. Attentive. Fun, yet steady as the Rocky Mountains she'd recently left behind. Why hadn't he ever gotten married? Had she messed that up for him? Or had he just not found the right one?

And why, oh, why, was she thinking about marriage right now? In the same thought as Hunter?

"And that's about it." Greg announced. "Other than that, we just want everyone to have fun. This is an out-reach night, so a lot of the kids have invited friends. We're hoping that once they feel at home here, they'll be willing to come back again on Sunday nights for youth group. And if anyone is interested in helping with the float for the Independence Day parade, Hunter and Rachel are heading that up on Wednesdays." Greg motioned in their direction, and Rachel jolted back to her windowsill perch, face warm, while Hunter lazily turned around to face the group. Why had she stayed that close to Hunter after they'd stopped talking? Embarrassing.

Just because Hunter was here and she hadn't expected him to be didn't change anything. Just because her heart had pitter-pattered at the sight of him didn't mean she had to worry. They were friends. That's why she was happy to see him.

Rachel had a plan for tonight that had nothing to do with the distracting shoulders in front of her. And, like Yoda, stick to it she would.

Chapter Eight

They were winning.

And so was Rachel. Behind the church was a sand volleyball court. And in the midst of a match, the teens had begun referring to her as *coach*. The word made her smile on so many levels, including deep in the part of her that secretly wondered if she was ever going to amount to anything. To be whoever God wanted her to be.

Rachel had thought of Olivia as her coach for years, because that's the role she'd played in Rachel's life in the beginning—on and off the court. It had taken Rachel a long time to call her Olivia or Liv. The fact that the kids were now referring to her with the same endearment and respect had Rachel feeling rather giddy.

Plus, there was Bree. She'd been on Rachel's team for the last hour, and they'd been taking down one competitor at a time. With each play, game and subsequent win, her face had lost another inch of scowl. She'd even smiled at Rachel a few times. Nothing raised a person's mood like winning.

They only had to score two more points to be named

lock-in volleyball champions. And when the ball hit the sand for the second time, the girls screeched and cheered. Rachel received a number of hugs, her hope soaring. Leave it to sports to be the glue that melted any concern over her.

Bree gave her a fist bump. No physical display from her. Which Rachel totally understood.

"Do you want to joust?"

Bree's question momentarily stole Rachel's words. She went with a casual "Sure," as an answer, attempting to keep her grin at an acceptable level. Anything more and the girl would be rolling her eyes.

The padded base and pedestals were set up in the middle of the parking lot. After waiting for a turn and donning the protective gear, they climbed up on the pedestals, each with a padded jousting pole in hand. The goal was to knock one's opponent down to the mat. Rachel took it easy on Bree while they jousted. They spent much of the time laughing. Both wore soft helmets, but she could still see Bree's eyes. They held a spark of competitiveness, but none of the malice she'd previously harbored.

Each of them knocked the other down once, and then, in the third round, Rachel gave some effort, but not enough to win. Bree sent her flying to the mat below. She stood, still laughing, and congratulated Bree.

A bunch of the teens had gathered around, and Hunter grinned at her from where he stood with a group of boys. She would have thought maybe, just maybe, he'd wear tennis shoes tonight in order to participate in the games. But no, his typical boots, jeans and faded T-shirt dress code was still intact.

The kids were yelling about something, and Rachel

glanced around, trying to figure out what had their excitement level increasing so quickly.

"Coach…" Bree took off the padded jousting helmet and tossed it onto the mat, and Rachel did the same with hers. "Are you going to do it?"

"Do what?"

"Joust with Hunter." A smile flashed. "I think you could take him down."

Ah. Rachel melted. The girl looked like whatever problems usually weighing her down had been put on hold for the evening.

Hunter had an eyebrow raised in challenge. "What do you say?"

"If you want to lose, I'm happy to joust with you."

The kids burst into laughter at her smack talk. Hunter grabbed the other jousting stick and inched close to her, lowering his voice. "Maybe you could give an actual effort this time?"

Oh, no, he didn't. "She's a kid." She matched her volume to his. "I was playing nice."

"I assume you won't have that same concern with me."

"You know what, McDermott? For once in your life, you're right."

Hunter had planned to go easy on Rachel, but she was pummeling him. He'd spent the last few minutes defending himself against her attacks. The hits were coming in fast and furious. They didn't hurt, just jostled him.

Had he wakened a beast?

One caught him on the left side. He lost his balance but managed to regain his footing.

Hunter took a swing at Rachel, planning to whack the jousting stick from her grip, but just as he was about to make contact, she wobbled and her body shifted forward. It was too late to change the point of impact. His stick connected with her noggin. Hard. Her head rocked to the side, and she flew off the pedestal. He was down beside her faster than he could count to two.

"Rach." Her eyes were open but dazed. She blinked numerous times. Even with their padded helmets on, that hit had rattled her. He removed her helmet and gently ran fingertips along her scalp, checking for a bump. "Are you okay?"

Her eyes filled with moisture that didn't spill. "I'm fine."

Tough girl. His sigh came out ragged—half relief, half exasperation. "You're not fine. I struck your head pretty hard."

Hunter removed his helmet, and she shifted as though she was trying to get up. He helped her to a sitting position.

"The world's a little spinny, but I'm fine."

Spinny wasn't a word. So *not* fine.

"I'll get some ice."

"No. I'll come."

Arguing with her—head injury or not—would be pointless.

Hunter supported her as she stood, keeping his arm around her. She wasn't completely herself because she didn't shove him away. Until they stepped down from the mat and their feet met the pavement. Then she pushed his arm off. "I'm fine."

Three "fines" didn't make it true.

He wasn't taking any chances of her crashing to the

parking lot and injuring herself more. Despite her pro-
tests, Hunter kept her tucked against him and leaned
down until his mouth met her ear. "Every kid and leader
here is watching you right now."

She peeked out from his T-shirt while he continued.
"And if you don't let me help you inside, I will pick you
up and carry you. And despite how strong you think
you are, I will win that tussle."

A gush of warm, frustrated air leaked out against
his chest.

"Fine."

Number four.

Greg jogged over, concern splitting his brow. "Is
she okay?" He touched Rachel's arm, and something
in Hunter flamed to life. Jealousy. Outrage. Protective-
ness. Any option worked. "How do you feel? Bree said
you took a blow to your head. She came flying over to
tell me."

A soft grin lifted Rachel's mouth. "She's a good kid."

Greg let out a relieved laugh. "She is, but right now
I need to make sure you're okay. Should we call an am-
bulance?"

"Absolutely not."

"Do you want someone to take you in to the clinic?"

"No," Rachel answered, head shaking, then she
winced and stopped the movement. "I think ice will
work. It's not that big of a deal. Better me than one of
the kids."

Hunter tightened his grip around Rachel's shoulder.
He might not like the circumstances that got them here,
but he sure didn't mind her being snug against him. And
when she actually stayed there? Without kicking? Better than a Cowboys win.

"I'll help her." At Greg's nod of acceptance, Hunter walked toward the church, prompting Rachel to move with him. Once inside, he dropped her off in the back of the sanctuary, and—in spite of her grumbling—had her lie in the last row of chairs. "I'll be right back."

He trucked down to the kitchen, bagged some ice, grabbed a cloth to wrap around it and then headed back upstairs. Amazingly, she'd stayed put. She must be more messed up than he'd thought.

He sat on the chair next to her head, and she opened her eyes while he tucked the ice on the side where he'd made impact.

"Thanks." Her eyes closed again.

With the lightest touch, he swept a strand of hair from her forehead. "You're welcome. I'm sorry I almost killed you."

She shook with laughter, and the gold R pendant on her necklace slipped behind her neck. "You're not *that* strong, cowboy."

That sounded like an endearment to him. His heart was a jumping bean while he was this close to her. Touching her as though he had the right to. He should back away. Give them both some space. His attraction to her right now was nowhere near the friendship level he'd committed to.

"It was an accident, you know. I was aiming for your jousting stick, but then you lost your balance and moved, and I nailed your head instead."

"So you're telling me you weren't even trying to knock me down. Thanks a lot. That makes it even worse."

Amusement tugged at his mouth. She was still his Rachel.

"Did you see Bree tonight? She's softening. Letting me in."

His fingers slid along her hairline again, and when she didn't complain or fight, he continued the soothing motion.

Do you see yourself? Talking to me like it used to be? "Yeah, I saw. You're good for her. For all of them."

"Thanks."

"That's three thanks in a row." Though one had been sarcastic. "I think we'd better take you in to the clinic."

"Ha."

"Seriously, Rach. I do need to know you're okay." He cupped a hand over her mouth, forcing himself to ignore the fact that he was *touching her lips*. "And, no, you're not *fine*." Begrudgingly, he let go.

After an audible sigh, she slid her phone out of her back pocket and held it up. "We can text Lucy and she can ask Graham. Does that work for you?"

"Sure."

Hunter got his phone from his pocket. Rachel rattled off Lucy's number and he sent a text explaining what had happened and asking Lucy to check with Graham about what they should do.

Rachel shifted to sit up in the chair next to him as Lucy's reply came back quickly. Is she okay???

She seems to be. She's talking and sitting up now, but I want to make sure.

First off, stare longingly into her eyes. Do that for at least five minutes and then get back to me.

He laughed. Leave it to Lucy to use this as an opportunity to make this about him and Rachel.

"What?" Rachel questioned.

"Nothing."

When Lucy had first moved to town, she'd figured out pretty quickly that he harbored feelings for Rachel—though they'd been masked under layers of upset and hurt. She'd often thrown him tidbits of information about Rachel over the years that he hadn't asked for, but had secretly appreciated. Though lately, thankfully, she'd quieted down on any matchmaking attempts.

Another text from Lucy came through.

Hang on, I'm checking.

"She's going to ask Graham."

"Okay." Rachel's head tipped his way, then landed on his shoulder. He froze. Something must seriously be wrong with her.

She smelled so good. He imagined it was her shampoo teasing his senses, but he didn't know for sure.

He inhaled. He wouldn't be this close to her again, maybe ever, so he might as well take advantage.

It's Graham. Did she lose consciousness?

"Did you black out at all, Rach?"

"Nope."

Is she disoriented? Stumbling? Slurred speech? Dazed?

Doesn't seem like it.

Anything abnormal you're noticing?

Huh. How to answer that question? Well, she's being unusually grateful and nice. Not her typical behavior.

Ha! Is she related to Lucy by blood??

Hunter chuckled.

"What? What is he saying?" At Rachel's exasperated tone, he glanced in her direction. Her eyes were open, and she shifted her head against his shoulder as though she might move. He held his breath, only starting up again when she didn't scoot away from him.

"He's just asking about you."

His phone beeped, and Hunter read Graham's questions aloud as they came through.

"Do you feel dizzy?"

"No."

"Ringing in your ears?"

"Nope."

After a few more questions with the same answer, Hunter started to relax.

I need you to look at her pupils. Check if they look bigger than normal (if you can tell) or if they're unequal sizes.

Again, laughter rumbled in his chest. So Lucy had been right. He did get to stare longingly into Rachel's eyes. He was torn. Part of him wanted the opportunity to be that close to her, but he also didn't want to leave his current position.

"Enough, McDermott. I don't know why me being injured is so amusing to you."

"It's not. Doc Redmond's just making me laugh." He set the phone on the chair to his right, then scooted her away from his shoulder so that they were face-to-face. "I'd never be okay with anything happening to you, Rach." Their close proximity made him pause and swallow. "It would kill me to know I'd seriously hurt you."

He'd done exactly that in the past. It had been emotional hurt that time around, but that was almost worse, in Hunter's opinion. Who was he kidding? Both options were unacceptable.

His hand had involuntarily moved to her arm, and she didn't move away from his touch. The warmth of her skin made his pulse skip like a scratched CD.

"What are you doing?" Her voice didn't hold her usual bite. Just curiosity.

"Checking your pupils."

He forced himself to ignore the fact that for the first time in six years, his lips were seconds away from hers. Made himself focus on her gorgeous eyes. He studied one, then the other. Compared. They seemed fine to him, but then again, he wasn't a doctor. But the pupil sizes matched, at least.

"I think they look okay." Although that wasn't a term he'd use to describe himself at the moment. He was not "fine" or "okay" or anything anywhere near that. He was a mess. He hadn't thought it was possible to want Rachel more than he had the day she'd left for college and taken his heart with her.

But he'd been wrong.

Chapter Nine

If she was okay, then why was Hunter's face still inches from hers? One of those instances where if either of them leaned forward their lips would be reintroduced.

Rachel's breathing shallowed out. His eyes were the color of maple syrup and, by the way they held her attention, just as sticky sweet. The usual scruff covered his cheeks—as if he'd shave when he got around to it— though she'd never witnessed him with an actual beard. He always hovered somewhere in between.

"Why don't you shave every day?"

"I don't know. Just easier, I guess." His voice was low, amused and wreaking havoc on her. "Are you telling me I should shave every day?"

"I don't care what you do. I'm just curious." She was prolonging their close proximity with stupid conversation. She couldn't actually want to be near him, could she? Maybe the blow to her head was making her crazy. After all, she'd just been tucked against Hunter's shoulder like she owned it. Like it was her personal spot to rest on. And, honestly, it had felt like a perfect fit. He was muscular, yet his shoulder had felt just right.

"4 for 4" MINI-SURVEY

We are prepared to **REWARD** you with 2 FREE books and 2 FREE gifts for completing our MINI SURVEY!

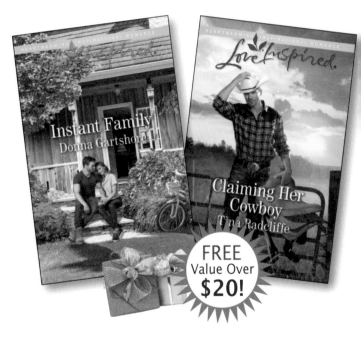

FREE
Value Over
$20!

You'll get...
TWO FREE BOOKS & TWO FREE GIFTS
just for participating in our Mini Survey!

Dear Reader,

IT'S A FACT: if you answer 4 quick questions, we'll send you 4 FREE REWARDS!

I'm not kidding you. As a leading publisher of women's fiction, we value your opinions… and your time. That's why we are prepared to **reward** you handsomely for completing our mini-survey. In fact, we have 4 Free Rewards for you, including 2 free books and 2 free gifts.

As you may have guessed, that's why our mini-survey is called **"4 for 4".** Answer 4 questions and get 4 Free Rewards. It's that simple!

Thank you for participating in our survey,

Pam Powers

To get your 4 FREE REWARDS:
Complete the survey below and return the insert today to receive 2 FREE BOOKS and 2 FREE GIFTS guaranteed!

"4 for 4" MINI-SURVEY

1 Is reading one of your favorite hobbies?
☐ YES ☐ NO

2 Do you prefer to read instead of watch TV?
☐ YES ☐ NO

3 Do you read newspapers and magazines?
☐ YES ☐ NO

4 Do you enjoy trying new book series with FREE BOOKS?
☐ YES ☐ NO

YES! I have completed the above Mini-Survey. Please send me my 4 FREE REWARDS (worth over $20 retail). I understand that I am under no obligation to buy anything, as explained on the back of this card.

☐ I prefer the regular-print edition
105/305 IDL GMYL

☐ I prefer the larger-print edition
122/322 IDL GMYL

FIRST NAME   LAST NAME

ADDRESS

APT.#   CITY

STATE/PROV.   ZIP/POSTAL CODE

She was stinking Goldilocks.

"Rach?"

"Yeah?"

He leaned forward and everything stood still. His lips pressed against her forehead and held before he eased back. Disappointment and relief tangoed in her gut.

"I'm really sorry I hurt you."

Tears surfaced but thankfully didn't fall. Was he referring to today or six years ago? Maybe all of the above.

"Hunter...about what you said a minute ago—I hope you know I wouldn't be okay if anything happened to you, either." And it was true. He might have scarred her way back when, but she would never wish him harm. He was a part of her past. And that made up the pieces of who she was now. Those months with him at the end of high school had been some of the softest of her life. She rarely opened up like that and probably hadn't since.

His fingers slid into the hair at the nape of her neck, and his lips trailed down from where they'd touched her forehead, landing on one cheekbone, then the other. Her lungs flat-out quit functioning. Amazing how her body could stay alive without oxygen.

What was he doing? He pressed a kiss lightly to her nose. She should tell him to stop. But in the last few seconds her body had turned to undercooked brownie batter. Soft. Warm. Compliant.

Surely he'd pull back now. Surely her eyes weren't refilling with tears at his gentleness. This was just about the fact that he'd injured her, wasn't it?

Rachel didn't even realize her eyes had closed until she thought to open them. His mouth was a whisper away from hers. Now's when she would end this. She'd already let things go too far. But when he'd brushed her hair from her forehead earlier and then continued the soothing motion, she'd melted. And she was having a hard time forming a backbone again. That thing that told her to retreat. To remember what had happened between them in the past. The gut-wrenching way he'd responded to her and shut her out. How it had hurt with a pain that had radiated through her body. How it had taken everything in her to walk away from him.

It didn't work the last time and it won't work this time. Nothing has changed for either of us. Plus, YOU'RE MOVING.

Her conscience might be screaming directives at her, but her stupid heart wasn't listening. Which was why, when Hunter's lips met hers with the slightest touch, she let it happen.

His hands were warm, gentle, as he eased her closer. She didn't fight it. How could she? She'd never been able to resist Hunter. That was part of the problem.

Rachel gave in to the kiss, and those symptoms he'd asked her about started happening in rapid succession. Dazed. Dizzy.

Somehow she'd gone from wanting to run to being a willing participant.

"Rachel, are you—" Greg's voice came from the back of the sanctuary. She wrenched back, managing to put a foot between herself and Hunter in one giant lurch.

Both of their heads snapped to Greg, and by the stunned look on his face, he'd witnessed their lip-lock. And why wouldn't he have? It wasn't like she'd been worrying about someone walking in on them. Nope. She'd just let herself go straight back to the land of immaturity. No thinking. Just feeling. And for a split second, it had almost felt worth it.

Greg didn't exactly look upset—though he had the right to be. She and Hunter were chaperones at a youth group lock-in, and they were the ones caught kissing. Her face flamed. What had she done? What was she thinking? And, seriously, how much brain damage had that jousting stick caused?

"You okay?"

She managed one nod to Greg's question, and then Hunter took over.

"We checked with Dr. Redmond. She doesn't have any of the symptoms he asked about." His voice didn't hold the same panic she felt coursing through her. Did anything ever upset him? The man was as calm as a lazy river or a hammock in the summer sun. She, on the other hand, felt more like the frayed edges of an old flag that had endured stormy weather for too long. "And if anything pops up, she'll be contacting him." Hunter's statement left no room for arguing. Rachel had no choice but to agree. Pretend she hadn't just thrown away all of the strides she'd made in the last six years in one idiotic moment.

Disappointment roared through Rachel as Greg walked toward them.

He was going to reprimand them. Rachel detested that feeling. Hated the knowledge that she'd let herself get here. And for what? It wasn't as though a relationship could happen between Hunter and her. They'd already had this conversation. Set the boundaries that she'd just flown right by without even blinking.

"I realize you guys are adults, but just..." Greg looked away, his face mirroring Rachel's discomfort.

"Not here, okay? If I'd been one of the kids walking in, that wouldn't have been good."

"You're right. I'm so sorry." Rachel stood. She wanted nothing more than to flee. "I'm going to go check on my girls." Because she was the best chaperone and should get back to it. Obviously. She reached the doors of the sanctuary and ran out before either Hunter or Greg could continue the most uncomfortable conversation *ever*.

Her head ached, but it wasn't from connecting with a jousting stick. It was from the certainty that she'd messed up. Big time.

This was why she hadn't wanted to be around Hunter in the first place. Why she avoided him whenever she came home. Because she couldn't make a mature decision when it came to him. Show the town how much she'd changed. Keep focused on the teens. Get to know Bree.

How'd that plan work out for her?

Rachel had taken a giant leap backward. She'd basically proved the opposite—that she was still the same girl. That scene with Hunter had been eerily similar to something she would have done in high school.

It had also landed her a warning from Greg and a heart dangerously close to losing its protective shell.

Hunter scrubbed a hand across the back of his neck. That hadn't gone well. It had for a few seconds, but then…back to reality. To possibly leaving things worse than when he'd first walked in here with Rachel.

"I'm sorry." He stood to face Greg. "That was completely inappropriate." Seriously. Who kissed someone while acting as a youth chaperone? Him, apparently.

He just hadn't been able to resist. Once his lips had touched Rachel's skin, he'd been as gone as a fly ball over left field.

They'd finally been in a good place—had managed a friendship after all of this time—and now he'd ruined it all with one impetuous kiss. And until he could talk to her and apologize, he'd just have to live with the question of how much he'd messed things up. Would it take another six years to make up for this?

And it didn't bode well for him, either, that she'd just been whacked in the head—by him—and he'd taken advantage of the situation. Yes, she'd seemed okay. Hadn't had any of the problems Doc Redmond had questioned them about, but that didn't make what he'd done right.

"Apology accepted," Greg responded. "I'm not one to hold a grudge. I'm actually quite a fan of grace."

"Makes sense, you being a pastor and all. It won't happen again." Unfortunately, ever. Hunter headed out of the row and met Greg as they walked to the back of the sanctuary.

"I'm guessing you wish I would have waited a few more minutes before barging in here to check on Rachel, aren't you?"

Amusement rose up. "In the spirit of honesty, that would have been helpful." Hunter pushed open the door, holding it for both of them. "You're a pastor. Are you even allowed to say something like that?"

Greg laughed. "Since I'm also human, yes, I am."

After heading back to the kids, they split up, leaving Hunter to deal with the repercussions of what had just happened. He knew better than to seek Rachel out right then. If he went anywhere near her anytime soon, he had no doubt she'd find one of the jousting sticks and take it to him. At this point, he needed to leave her alone until after the lock-in, at least. Maybe longer.

But the persistent thought running through his mind—the one he'd really like to dismiss—was, why hadn't Rachel flinched from his kiss? Backed away? Slapped him? Instead, she'd been with him every step of the way. After the slightest hesitation, she'd been all-in.

That plagued him the most. Because that was the Rachel he used to love. She was high and low, and sweet and snarky, and everything about her surprised him in the best way. She used to kiss him like that. Like she needed him as much as he needed her.

If Hunter let himself dream, he could picture Rachel staying in this town. The two of them married. They'd have the occasional fight, and she'd win. No doubt. And he'd be fine with that—as long as he got to keep her. But eventually she would question if she'd chosen the wrong fork in the road. Just like his mom. Even his imagination didn't provide a happy ending to that tale.

On his tenth birthday, Hunter had been missing his mother. She might have been half a mom, she might not have been the most present, but she'd been his. He'd sneaked into his dad's bedroom, tucked into his mom's side of the bed and allowed himself some tears. Then he'd opened the drawer of her bedside table, hoping to find—what, he didn't know. Something to remind him of her. To comfort. He'd come across a letter in his father's handwriting. Worn, as though it had been reread numerous times. He'd put it back in the drawer and tried to ignore it. But after a minute, he'd caved. Pieces of it would forever be ingrained in his memory.

Please don't leave us. I love you. We need you. Stay with us.

That was when Hunter understood why his father had turned so bitter. He'd begged his wife to stay, and she hadn't. That knowledge had hurt on so many levels. More than Hunter had been able to comprehend at that age.

His mom had never been happy on the ranch. And when his father had asked her to stay and she'd still left, it had shattered his dad. But instead of becoming sad and broken, Dad had turned hard. He'd shut down.

Hunter had never admitted to his father that he'd gone snooping that day—and that really hadn't been his intent. But the words, the pain of that letter and his mom's reaction had stayed with him all of this time. The roots of that discovery had grown deep in him. Hunter had come to the conclusion that his dad should never have convinced his mom to marry him in the first place. To live a life she didn't want.

He believed his mom had tried to be there for them. That more than a few of the tears she'd cried had been over the fact that she'd wanted to connect with him and Autumn, but could never quite cross the chasm. He'd gone to his friends' houses. He remembered gathering around supper tables, the way parents would tease each other, laugh and hug their children. Those things had happened sparingly in his home. There had been days Mom hadn't gotten out of bed. Some snapping and moments she'd lose her temper. Apologies and more tears after. By the time she left, he'd forgotten what it meant to hope.

Hunter refused to repeat any of that scenario with Rachel.

She'd been very clear with him about what she wanted, and it wasn't this town. Or to live on a ranch. Or even with him. Which was why he would never again ask her to stay.

Even if it took everything in him not to.

Chapter Ten

On Tuesday evening, Rachel sat on her front porch swing, waiting for Bree. She had a book to pass the time, but so far she hadn't made it through one page. Bree's text had come in about fifteen minutes ago.

Are you busy? I need to talk to someone.

I'm at home. Want to stop by? Rachel had included directions in the text and Bree had responded that she'd be over shortly.

Rachel was over the moon that Bree had reached out to her, but worried about what could be wrong. Was it her parents? Or an issue with a friend?

She prayed for wisdom to know how to best be there for Bree.

It had been an interesting last few days since the lock-in. Not a lot of contact from Hunter, which Rachel was just fine with. She felt absolutely no need to revisit their foolish kiss. Though she had beaten herself up over the infraction. Hunter had texted on Saturday to check on how she was feeling. She'd replied that her head was fine. No concussion symptoms. And then she'd told him that he should stop worrying and feeling guilty. His retort of *I'm just glad you're not going to file a lawsuit* had made her laugh.

And then, to add to the eventful weekend, Rachel had come home after church on Sunday to find an unexpected guest on her porch. A speckled Great Dane. No sign of where the animal had come from. No collar or tags. Rachel had given him some water to drink and then fed him. She'd tried to get him to come inside that night, but he'd balked. On Monday morning, she'd opened her front door to find him asleep on her porch. When the shelter had opened, she'd called, but they hadn't had a record of anyone searching for a lost dog matching his description.

They'd also been out of space. So she'd done something stupid. She'd said she would keep him for a bit. Until they had room. Rachel had started calling him Moose because his long legs reminded her of that animal, and every dog needed a name, even if it was only temporary.

Moose rose from his resting spot to her right, gave a squeaky yawn and stretched, then came to sit in front of the swing.

Rachel scrubbed behind his ears. "You're such a good boy. I think somebody is missing you." She hadn't used a leash to keep him at her place, but in the last three days, he'd stuck close by. Perhaps the dog food she'd bought for him had something to do with it. For such a large animal, Rachel would expect him to be rambunctious. Knock things around and cause a ruckus. But he was more partial to snoozing. She'd rinsed him down this morning—he'd been dirty as all get-out—but he'd need a real bath one day soon.

Once he found new owners. Or his current ones. "You can crash here for a little bit, big guy, but don't get too comfortable because I'm not staying much longer." She gazed into his mournful eyes, hopefully communicating dog speak, wondering who she was reminding—herself or Moose.

Dust rose up from a vehicle coming down her drive. Bree.

The girl parked and walked up the steps. She wore denim boyfriend capris and a striped short-sleeved shirt, her strawberry blond hair down in loose, beachy curls. Moose greeted her with some sniffing, a few licks and one *roo-roo*—as if saying hello. His intrusion broke through the gloomy fog surrounding Bree, and she fleetingly brightened.

"Did you get a dog?"

"No." Rachel shook her head with a vengeance.

Bree eyed the stainless steel water and food bowls that were stationed at the shady end of the porch—also necessary purchases.

"Are you dog sitting?" She sat next to Rachel on the swing, and Moose followed. Bree rubbed her fingertips along his head and back, giving in to his obvious plea for attention. After a few seconds, he settled on the strip of porch in front of them.

"Something like that. He's a stray. I'm just keeping him until the shelter finds his owners or has room for him."

Moose looked up at her with hurt in those big dark eyes.

What? I told you I'm leaving. You should have lis-

tened and not started getting attached. Advice Rachel could also give to herself regarding so many things. Hunter, for one. The girl next to her on the swing. Even this town was growing on her.

"So, tell me what's going on."

"My dad is moving to Austin." Bree's words came out in a rush, like water bubbling over the edge of a boiling pot. "I know it's not that far away, but…" Her voice dipped. Wobbled. For a second, Rachel thought the tears pooling in her eyes would spill, but Bree blinked them back. "He didn't even ask me or my younger sister our opinions. Just told us he got a new job. We get to visit him on weekends." Sarcasm spewed from every pore. "Because that's what I want to do on the weekend— leave my friends to stay in another town with my jerk of a dad in some apartment."

"That really stinks. I'm sorry." Rachel let the words rest for a second, wishing she could find a way to make it better. But sometimes life just wasn't easy.

She contemplated what to say before speaking. "I don't know your dad, obviously, but maybe he's just looking for a new start. Maybe he has no idea how upsetting this is to you. Do you think he would listen if you talked to him about it?"

Bree's shoulders inched up, then drooped as though carrying a massive weight. The faint creak of the swing's chain filled the otherwise tranquil evening. "Maybe." Her answer came out softly. Filled with very little hope. "I guess it's worth a shot."

"What about your mom? Have you talked to her about it?"

The girl's head shook.

"I understand that speaking to your parents about

all of this is hard and probably uncomfortable. I get it. But I know from experience that it's better to say something now than to wish you had after the fact." Rachel had learned that lesson at a young age. On the morning of her parents' deaths, she'd fought with her mom over something so stupid—when she could have a cell phone. How all of the other kids had them, except for her. She'd screamed and raged and slammed her bedroom door. She'd been a typical teenager—so she'd been told. But the rest of the story wasn't normal.

Before they'd left for the cattle auction, her dad had come into her room. He'd always been so good to her. Calm and loving and patient. He'd hugged her. Told her everything was going to be okay, and that once she calmed down, she should apologize to her mother.

They'd left, and Rachel had known immediately that she should make amends. But instead of calling, she'd waited. Let her anger continue a little longer.

She would apologize later, she'd decided.

But not everyone got a later.

Her parents had never come home again. The car accident that had taken their lives had seen to that.

"Before my mom died, we fought. It was an unnecessary argument. Totally my fault. I had the opportunity to call her and say I was sorry, and I didn't."

Sympathy moisture pooled in Bree's eyes.

"I've worked through it now. Someone—" *Olivia* "—helped me back in high school." Rachel had come to understand that her mom had loved her. That a disagreement and Rachel's immature behavior wouldn't change that. And knowing her mother, she could accept that truth—the kind of limitless love her mom had had for her. "But if I could go back and do it differently, I would. Not that your situation is the same as mine, but I think it applies. Your parents don't have any idea how you're feeling, and they won't unless you talk to them. You still may not end up with some perfect scenario, but it might give you some peace."

Bree nodded contemplatively. She pressed the toes of her simple green sandals against the porch, sending the swing into motion. "Thank you for sharing that about your mom. It helps that you're not just telling me what to do without backing it up."

Rachel's mouth curved. "I was the same way as a teenager. I needed the real deal. No canned advice for me."

"Right?" Bree laughed. "Adults should realize that we can sniff out the fake stuff."

"I couldn't agree with you more."

They stayed on the swing for a while after that. Talking some. Sitting in silence for part of it.

Before Bree left, Rachel prayed for her.

The girl's walk down the steps was less dejected than her way up. She even waved right before she got into her car and gave a relatively cheerful, "Thanks, Coach."

In the land of teenagers, Rachel would call that a victory.

The next night, Rachel drove to Hunter's thirty minutes before the youth would show up to work on the float so she could help set up. She wore an old, long volleyball T-shirt that had her name and number scrawled across the back over capri leggings. Last week her cute ruffled shirt had gotten a hole in it, and Rachel wasn't about to sacrifice another piece of her favorite clothing.

She'd been tempted to arrive right at seven to avoid

alone time with Hunter, but she was determined to do everything as she typically did.

She hoped if she ignored that their kiss had occurred, it would blow over and they could go back to the good place they'd been in. Hopefully Hunter wouldn't bring it up. But what was there to even say?

The two of them had been done a long time ago. They wanted different things, and one rogue kiss wasn't going to change that.

Hunter had only asked about her supposed injury since the lock-in. He hadn't brought up anything else. Which meant maybe he wanted the same thing as her—to just move forward as friends per their original conversation.

Which would be perfect, because then Rachel wouldn't have to delve into why she'd let the kiss happen in the first place.

When she entered the barn, Hunter was dragging out the large plastic totes. Tonight the group would adhere the fake grass to the trailer and then mount the other props they'd crafted. The youth would be excited to see the float finally take shape.

"Cowboy." She greeted him when she reached his side.

Hunter's dimples flashed as he nodded hello. "Teen whisperer."

They fell into a rhythm as they set up. No talking. No awkwardness. Relief skipped along Rachel's spine. Maybe they really were going to just let the kiss slide into the past. They could add it to the pile of their history together.

Hunter wore a simple white T-shirt tonight. The kind that came out of a three-pack and shouldn't look so good on someone. If Rachel tried to wear something like that, she'd resemble a box. Hunter could star in their ad. He even smelled good—something yummy and masculine.

This whole being friends gig would be a lot easier if he wasn't so stinking attractive.

At least, that's what she told herself.

When Rachel ran out of things to prep, she panicked. There was still fifteen minutes left before the kids would start trickling in. Far too much time for an unapproved conversation to sprout.

"What else do we need to do?" *Please, please keep me occupied. Give me a job.* Something. Anything. Perhaps she could volunteer to go check on the cattle.

"Think that's it." Hunter placed the last of the staple guns on the trailer.

"Did I tell you I found a dog camped out on my porch?" Of course the answer was no. Rachel caught him up on the appearance of Moose. "He even slept inside last night, which he wouldn't do at first. I put a rug by the front door for him, but in the middle of the night, he curled up on the floor by my bed." Relaying that story to Hunter ate up all of two minutes. *Moose, why couldn't you have caused some kind of trouble?* Then she would have been able to fill more time.

"That's crazy no one has reported him as missing yet. Though it's not a bad idea for you to have a dog for protection since you're living by yourself." And now Hunter sounded like her brother. His eyes narrowed slightly. "I'm actually a little shocked that you're here tonight."

"Why?"

"I just wasn't sure if you were ever going to talk to me again."

What? It wasn't as if he'd been knocking down her door. "I haven't heard from you except for the texts on Saturday, so maybe you're avoiding me, McDermott."

"Not avoiding." Hunter clarified. "Giving you space. There's a difference."

"Is there?"

"Yes, Your Sassiness."

Rachel planned to stick with humor. If she kept replying with sarcasm, she'd exasperate Hunter, and then maybe he'd give up on having this little chat.

"As to your earlier comment and whether I *want* to talk to you again, I'd have to go with maybe." Rachel tapped a finger to her lips as though contemplating. "Probably." She stretched the word out.

"Are you ever not going to be snarky when I ask you a question?"

"It's unlikely."

A sigh leaked from him. "That's the answer I expected. I don't suppose you're ready to talk about what happened at the lock-in yet."

"I already told you my head is absolutely fine."

"That's not what I mean and you know it."

Why did Hunter have to push? Why couldn't he let it go? Ever since she'd been home, people—including Hunter—had been infiltrating her life.

The other day, Val had pulled out of Rachel that Hunter had kissed her. It had been like extracting a tooth, but still. And then her friend had responded with a sympathetic, "What are we going to do about this?"

Rachel had almost burst into tears at the "we." While she'd been away, she'd forgotten what that felt like. Ever since she'd been back in Fredericksburg, *we* was exactly what she'd experienced. Hunter and everyone helping on the house. The church needing her. The boys and Cash and Liv thankful to have her home. Drawing her in like a toasty blanket on a cold, dreary day.

That *we* was exactly what scared her, though. She remembered the *we* of being a family. A real one. With a mom and dad who loved her. A brother who both tormented, annoyed and delighted her. One who wasn't her guardian but just a sibling.

But she knew *we* didn't last.

Rachel broke it. She always wrecked things. Relationships. That last fight with her mom—no matter how many times she forgave herself, it haunted her. Hearts, like she had with Hunter.

That's why Rachel was careful. Kept people at a distance, sometimes without even realizing what she was doing. Only her family and Val had slipped in through the cracks. And now Hunter, once again.

Hadn't he learned well enough the last time? Why did he even want to be around a broken piece of glass like her? Didn't he know her jagged edges would cut him? If he'd started hoping for something between them after their kiss, he'd be disappointed. Again. She was still planning to move. That hadn't changed.

"Listen, Hunter, there's nothing that needs to be said. We're adults. It happened. It shouldn't have. End of story."

After Rachel delivered her verdict on their relationship—unwilling to discuss anything deeper than surface level, of course—she had the audacity to pick up a staple gun as if she planned to get to work.

But Hunter wasn't done. Whether Rachel wanted to

or not, they were going to hash this out. He took the staple gun from her hand and set it back on the trailer.

"We're talking about this."

A scowl cut through her forehead. "We already did."

"That wasn't a conversation, Rach. That was a one-woman conclusion. I was part of what happened too, you know."

Wide eyes greeted him. "Trust me, I know." Her arms crossed. "You want to discuss it here?" She glanced around the empty barn.

The kids wouldn't show up for another ten minutes, so, yes. Here. Now. Those were Hunter's choices.

Based on Rachel's deflection since she'd arrived, Hunter would guess she'd prefer never.

The woman was good at steering clear when something made her uncomfortable. Five days had passed since the lock-in. He'd given her plenty of room, and he was done waiting.

"Why? Do you need a fancier place to hold a conversation?"

"No. Of course not. But there's nothing that needs to be said. We'll just put it aside. Pretend it didn't happen."

"Rach." His voice was low, gravelly. Hurt, confusion and remorse all swirled between them.

Her demeanor softened. She lost a bit of the act. "We're okay, Hunter."

Were they? He didn't think so. But he'd been praying awfully hard over the last few days that they would be.

"I have something I need to say to you."

She didn't speak. Just waited.

"I promised you could trust me, and then I broke that with the kiss. I'm sorry."

She twisted the toe of one flip-flop into the dirt,

her bright orange polish gaining a layer of dust with the movement. Rachel memorized the ground for what felt like years. Finally she looked up. "I *do* still trust you. Besides, it wasn't just you. We both participated."

The temptation to let that thought warm him was strong, but he shook it off. Hunter didn't need the reminder. He'd thought about that fact plenty in the last few days. "I know. I just… I don't want to lose you over this. I don't want us to go back to fighting or not talking or avoiding. I like being friends with you."

"You're not going to lose me." The way she held eye contact with him gave him hope she was telling the truth. "You're not." And the secondary declaration helped, too. "Believe it or not, McDermott, you're actually starting to grow on me."

The tension that had been thrumming through him for days began to ebb.

"I am hard to shake."

"Exactly." Contemplation furrowed her brow. "Like a leech. Or a wasp that won't stop buzzing around my head."

She was back to joking around, but he was okay with that now that he'd said what he needed to. "Promise we're good?"

"Promise."

Pent-up air leaked from his lungs. "I feel better. Aren't you relieved I made you talk about this?"

Her mouth curved. "No."

"Stubborn. You can't just admit it, can you? You could give our bull a run for his money."

"Did you just compare me to a bull?" Her nose wrinkled, and the humor dropped from her face as her gaze flitted past him like butterfly wings. "I don't know why it matters so much to you, anyway." The words were so quiet, he almost didn't catch them.

Felt like she was really asking why *she* mattered so much to him.

A question he was tempted to answer. To tell her he'd always cared about her. Always would. But Hunter couldn't go there. Couldn't unravel all of that. His original thought in pursuing a friendship with Rachel was not to turn out like his father. Not to repeat those mistakes. And he was light-years ahead of his old man in that regard. Hunter clung to that right now, unwilling to let it be about anything more with Rachel. She was still planning to move, so it couldn't be. "It just does."

There. He'd just have to leave it at that. But he couldn't resist at least attempting to erase her look of sadness.

"Besides, if I didn't have you in my life, who would torment me?"

She rolled her eyes and whacked him on the arm, making his chest shake with amusement. He wasn't sure he'd truly relaxed since their kiss. The fear that he'd ruined it all had been ruling him. But they were okay again. He wasn't going to lose her over one impetuous decision.

By the light in her eyes, his teasing seemed to be working, so he kept it up. "I'm not sure what I was thinking, trying to keep our relationship intact. I mean, you call me names. You don't even make any home-cooked meals for me, which I'm pretty sure would be a sign of a true friendship. And you're always hitting me." He rubbed the spot where she'd just done that very thing, acting as though she'd wounded him.

"You're a dork." Her tone was as dry as sawdust.

"See! This is what I'm talking about."

Her laughter stitched him back together, and peace rushed in. She might have been worried at first that he'd wanted more than the platonic relationship they'd agreed upon, but he'd talked her down. He—and God—had fixed it. Got them back to the good place they'd been in before he'd kissed her.

Hunter wasn't about to analyze why he was so concerned about losing Rachel when he knew that very thing was going to happen one day soon.

Tonight he was just going to rest in the knowledge that she was still in his life, even if he felt the limited time with her slipping like sand through his fingers.

Chapter Eleven

The sun hung low in the sky as Rachel drove home, and she flipped her visor down as she made the final turn. The last two days had passed in a blur.

After her talk with Hunter on Wednesday night, she'd gotten a phone call from Dana, calling about an interview. The board had narrowed the candidates down to Rachel and one other person. So on Thursday she'd driven to Houston, and this morning she'd had the interview.

Rachel thought—or hoped—it had gone well. Tough questions had been lobbed at her, but she'd never felt as though she was drowning without an answer to hold on to. The conversation had given her confidence that the school board would have her back if she landed the job, and the whole experience had only made her more confident it was the right opportunity for her.

Which conflicted with the rest of her emotions. Because she'd missed home. Had she really started to think of Fredericksburg as that again? Despite her attempts not to, she'd felt the absence of her friends and family in the short time she'd been gone. Her nephews' sweet dispositions. Hunter.

That last name made her stomach twist with concern. She couldn't miss him. Both of them knew she planned to move if she got the job. But she also conveniently hadn't told him about the interview. It had felt too raw. Too soon after they were finding their friendship footing again.

It was okay she hadn't mentioned it to him, right? If they were in a relationship, she would have. But they weren't. She hadn't done anything wrong in not telling Hunter about the interview. Who knew if she'd even get the job? Rachel wasn't one to count chickens before they'd hatched.

Last night, she and Dana had shopped and gone out to dinner. It had been wonderful, confirming what Rachel loved about the city. But being in Fredericksburg had begun to cloud her thinking. She'd started to enjoy the peace and quiet, and look forward to the mornings when she'd sit on her porch swing and do her devotions. Drink a cup of coffee before heading over to Cash and Liv's. It had become the perfect beginning to her day, and she couldn't imagine giving it up.

When she'd first arrived back in town, she'd expected to hate every minute of the summer. But instead, she'd had plenty of good flood her life.

Up and down her emotions swung, like a yo-yo in a child's hands.

On Wednesday night, when she'd left the barn to take the phone call from Dana, she'd confirmed the details of the interview and then turned to find Bree standing behind her, her features an open wound.

"You're leaving?" Bree had questioned.

Rachel had moved slowly toward the girl, not wanting her to scram before she could explain. She'd assumed the kids knew her plans—that she was only back for the summer—but had they ever had that conversation?

"Bree, this job has been in the works for months. I thought you knew my move home was temporary."

"Yeah, I knew that, but I thought..." The girl's demeanor had hardened like chiseled stone. None of the soft, almost-there tears from the evening before had remained. "Never mind what I thought." Her arms had wrapped around her stomach as if forming a shield. "It doesn't matter."

Bree mattered, but what could Rachel do about it? She really wanted this job. But at the same time, she cared about the teens. Her family. Hunter. And that dog on her porch. She hadn't planned to fall for this place— these people—but she had. And then, this morning, she'd talked to the board about leaving them all.

Her phone rang, and Rachel checked the caller ID. She didn't recognize the number but answered, anyway.

"This is Rachel."

"Rachel, this is Lisa Trupe from the board." Pandemonium erupted within Rachel's rib cage. Should she rejoice or grab the box of tissues from the backseat? "We just finished meeting, and we'd like to offer you the position. Everyone thinks you'll be a great fit. We wanted to let you know before the weekend so you could think about it and hopefully get back to us by Monday or Tuesday next week."

Months of stress rolled from Rachel's back. She'd put so much of her hope into this.

"Thank you so much, Lisa, but I don't need time

to think about it." Did she? Hadn't she wanted this all along? Rachel had never doubted this was where God was directing her. But then, why did the thought of leaving Hunter fill her with sorrow?

She might want it all, but that wasn't how life worked. She couldn't have Hunter and the job. And that was assuming he was even still interested in her.

No. She couldn't let the thought of their renewed relationship sway her. Besides, Hunter had apologized for their kiss. He hadn't confessed any feelings for her. Rachel knew what she needed to do.

"Are you sure?"

"Yes, I'm sure. I would love to accept the position." Rachel answered emphatically, as though the strength of her voice could erase any remaining concerns and doubts.

They talked details for another minute, then disconnected. If this was what she wanted, then why was her stomach churning? She couldn't tell if it was nerves, excitement or dread.

The thought of telling Hunter about the job heightened that last emotion. She'd grown used to having him in her life again. If something came up, Hunter was on the top of her list of people to call. But what would her accepting the job do to them? How would he handle it?

She could wait a few days to spill the news to him, couldn't she? Take some time to let the decision sink in and figure out what to say.

Rachel pulled down her drive, and when she neared the house, her headlights illuminated a truck sitting next to her Jeep's parking spot. Hunter's.

What was he doing here? So much for time to process how to tell him.

Moose popped up from his resting place and moseyed down the front steps while she rolled into her spot and turned off the ignition. He greeted her with a *roo-roo* when she opened her door. "Hey, boy. I missed you, too." She ran her hands over his soft head and ears. Cash and Grayson had been checking on him while she was gone. Which meant Moose had likely had his fair share of treats over the last two days.

Rachel grabbed her overnight bag, slipped her fingers through the straps of her heeled sandals and crossed the grass barefoot. The dog moved back up the porch steps and walked toward the swing. And that's when Rachel saw Hunter slouched over in it, sleeping.

Moose sniffed along his jeans and down to his boots as if to show Rachel they had an intruder and he'd done a good job being a watch dog. Most likely he'd *watched* Hunter come up the steps and accepted a rubdown before both of them had conked out.

The warmth of the previously sun-kissed wood met her soles as she walked up the steps. At Moose's intrusion, Hunter opened his eyes and propped himself up. "Hey." His warm eyes met hers.

"Hey." She set her overnight bag and shoes by the front door, and he glanced around as if getting his bearings.

"Been here awhile?"

He nodded. "Fell asleep." His grin was sheepish. Adorable. "Obviously." He scrubbed a hand through his hair, and the dark blond strands stuck up in handsome disarray.

"Did we…" Her fingers found her gold R necklace and toyed with the pendant. "Did we have plans I forgot?"

"Nope. I just got done working and thought maybe

you'd want to hang out. Grab dinner, catch a movie or go listen to some music in town. But then I sat down to wait for you, and…" He shrugged.

Rachel plopped onto the swing next to him, her decision to take the job weighing her down like a boulder strapped to her back. Hunter studied her, questioning, and everything in her wanted to lean in. Rest her head on his shoulder. Tell him how she suddenly felt confused about the job she wanted so badly, and it was all because of him.

What she wouldn't give for them to want the same things.

"You okay? What's wrong?" He laid an open hand on his jeans-clad leg, and like a fool, she put hers in it.

This man. What was she going to do with him? Even worse, what was she going to do without him?

She had to tell him. Rip off the Band-Aid. They were good, right? Surely they'd stay there. He would understand. He'd known all along this was her plan.

They both had.

Dread curled through Hunter as Rachel pushed her foot against the porch and set the swing in motion. Something was wrong. He could feel the tension coming from her, wrapping around him like a boa constrictor slithering around his chest.

"Were you out to dinner?" And, if yes, who had she been with?

"No."

He wasn't sure whether to feel relief or concern. When he'd opened his eyes a minute ago, her outfit had felt like a sucker punch. A fancy sleeveless shirt. Dress pants that ended just above her ankles. High heels hooked in her fingertips. A bright blue, chunky beaded necklace in addition to the gold one she usually wore. Light pink sparkly polish on her toenails. His first thought was that she'd been on a date, and he'd been sleeping on her porch waiting for her. He'd wanted to kick himself.

So, if she wasn't at dinner, hopefully that meant she hadn't just been on a date. Not that he was allowed to care about that stuff. Not with their rules and relationship-defining decisions. But if she wasn't going to date him, he sure wasn't okay with her going out with someone else. Not that they'd ever had that discussion.

"So where were you?"

She stared straight forward as night fully descended and the first few stars began twinkling. It reminded him of one of Kinsley's drawings—a smattering of light in the midst of a black sheet of construction paper. "I was in Houston."

His lungs morphed into a balloon with a pinprick, the air slowly leaking out. "For the job?"

She nodded.

And she hadn't told him.

Maybe he'd rather hear she'd been on a date. Another guy he could fight and contend with, but the job? Not a chance. His feelings for her might be growing, but he couldn't give them wings.

He tried with everything in him to remember he wanted this for her. "What happened?"

"They interviewed me again this morning."

He was having a hard time taking a full breath, so he counted on the shallow, painful ones to pull him through.

"And they offered me the job." She'd been looking at

her tan bare feet as she spoke, but now her gaze lifted to him, those green embers filled with more emotion than he could decipher. "I accepted."

It took him a minute to speak. "Congratulations." His voice cracked and he cleared his throat. "When do you leave?"

"The Monday after the parade."

A week and a half. Now it was his turn to stare out at the ranch. He'd known all along what her plans were, but that didn't fix the ache that had started right between his ribs.

He looked down at their hands. They were still touching. He'd offered her his hand as a comfort—at least, that's what he'd told himself—and she'd accepted. But now the simple gesture felt too intimate.

He needed to get out of here. Rachel was looking at him with wounded eyes—as if this was a choice *he'd* made—and he couldn't form the right words or thoughts.

Hunter stopped the swing and stood, the comforting warmth of her sitting beside him instantly gone. "I'm happy for you, Rach. I know how badly you wanted this." If he sounded rote, so be it. He was doing his best.

"Thanks." Her quiet response barely registered.

He felt a bit like a child who'd just had the ice cream on his cone fall to the dusty ground after his parent had warned him that very thing was about to happen. He should have expected this. She'd prepared him all along.

"You want to watch a movie?" She motioned inside. "Not that I have that much comfortable furniture...or we could play a game instead. I mean, you came over to do something, right?"

"I gotta—" *Get out of here.* He rubbed a hand across

the back of his neck. "I have some things I need to do."
Right. Even though he'd just been waiting for her for
how long? But at this point, he didn't care about logic.

For once, it was him who needed to escape.

The next few days crept by with only one consistency: no Hunter. No contact from him on Saturday.
At church on Sunday, Rachel somehow didn't see him.
By that night, her curiosity at his lack of presence or
texts was growing. And by Monday morning, she was
thoroughly confused. Almost angry.

Hunter had said they were fine—that they were
friends. But were they? Then where was he? Had her
taking the job messed with their relationship?

He couldn't just disappear from her life without
warning. He'd promised her a friendship and that's
what she expected.

Rachel had stayed on the swing long after he'd left
on Friday night, thinking. Praying. Hoping and trusting that she'd made the right decision about the job.

If she took Hunter out of the equation, she'd feel excitement. He was the one person making her question
her choice. Well…him and her family. Val. And the
teens. But the fact remained, no matter how close she'd
grown to any of them, she still didn't want this life.

Being in Houston had been so refreshing. The city
was bustling. Yes, she'd missed the quiet of the country. She'd missed her swing and being at peace with her
thoughts. There was a lot pulling her here. But there
was also a lot drawing her away.

Rachel busied herself all day Monday with Grayson
and Ryder. But when she arrived home in the evening,
the empty house haunted her. She felt…lonely. And

that's when she knew what was happening. She missed Hunter. She missed him, and she hadn't even left yet.

Rachel could contact him. Or she could do the smart thing and start putting some space between them. Not let any more feelings grow in the short remaining time she would be home.

She paced the few steps from one side of her living room to the other, then threw her arms into the air with a groan of annoyance. Enough of this. She changed into workout shorts and a tank, snagged her running shoes and laced up, then tore out of the house.

Moose didn't even pretend to be interested in joining her. He gave one bark as she took off and tried to outrun her frustrations.

She was leaving.

Hunter had been reeling from the news for three days now. Rachel's announcement on Friday had sent him into a tailspin.

He'd come to a very unsettling conclusion over the last few days—one he hadn't wanted to admit, even to himself. Despite all of his attempts not to, he'd developed feelings for Rachel again. Or, more likely, they'd never truly gone away. They ran like a deep and wide river inside of him. A current he couldn't turn off. He'd tried over the years. Even convinced himself he'd accomplished that very thing. But the reason there'd been so much angst between them after she'd left was because he'd never stopped caring for her.

And sometime in the last few weeks, he'd started hoping she might change her mind about moving and want to stay. He hadn't even realized the hope had started flickering until it had been abruptly snuffed out when she'd told him she'd taken the job.

He half snorted, half laughed at his naïveté. What had he expected? She'd been very honest about the fact that she planned to leave from the first moment she'd stepped foot in this town.

Since Friday night, he'd been a mess. Trying to regroup and figure out how to get his feelings under control. He'd been working himself to the bone, thinking manual labor might dull the ache of his new discovery. Hadn't worked yet.

Hunter had come in from the ranch tonight and showered, then thrown on some clean jeans, socks and a navy blue T-shirt. Now he strode over to his fridge and rummaged inside. Leftovers would suffice for dinner. He heated up beef Stroganoff and took the bowl over to the island. His elbows landed on the countertop as he bowed his head for a quick prayer, then dug in.

When a knock sounded on his door, he didn't bother getting up. "Come in," he called out, scooping the last bite into his mouth before turning.

Rachel stood in the open doorframe. Hunter swallowed, then clamped his jaw to keep it from falling open. He scrubbed a hand over his face to make sure he didn't have any food hitching a ride and popped up from the bar stool, walking toward her. He wanted to crush her in a hug. He wanted to tell her he'd missed her over the last few days. Instead, he said, "Hey." Brilliant.

She was wearing a colorful tank top, black running shorts and tennis shoes.

Her breathing seemed labored.

"Did you run here?"

"Yep."

"You want to sit? Glass of water?"

"Sure."

He went into the kitchen while she crossed to the couch. He filled a glass and handed it off to her, then sat on the love seat, not trusting himself to sit next to her.

"I've never really seen your house. Besides when I picked you up. And then you were so crabby it took all of my effort and attention just to get you out of here." She flashed a sassy grin and scanned the first floor.

The kitchen and island were open to the living room. Upstairs he had three bedrooms. Three. Who knew what for? He'd thought for a family one day. With the way things were going, maybe he could use one as a craft room. He would have plenty of time in the rest of his unmarried life to take up a hobby. Knitting. Crochet. Scrapbooking.

"It's really nice."

"Thanks."

What was she doing here? Had she come with another announcement to throw his world off-kilter?

Her legs bounced, and she jumped up from the couch and walked along the island, then went back to her seat and dropped onto the cushions.

"Rach, what's on your mind?"

Surprise tugged on her features. "Nothing. I was just…out for a run."

Didn't ring true, but Rachel wouldn't give up information easily. She might not even know what she was upset about.

He'd always been good at getting her to spill, much like she'd done with him.

His heart squeezed. His Rachel, with all of the walls and hurt and toughness. She tried to keep up appearances. Act as if life hadn't thrown really hard things at her. As though she could handle it all. But he knew her inside and out. And now he'd broken through. She might not be staying, but he'd chipped away at her defenses until she'd let him in. She might not love him, but she liked him. She'd come to him.

Now he just needed to figure out why.

"I can't believe you went running in this heat."

"Me, either."

"Come on." He stood, offered her a hand. When she accepted, he pulled her up, too. "I'll drive you home. But first I have somewhere to take you."

Chapter Twelve

"Where are we going?"

Rachel's annoyance filled the cab of his truck as Hunter made the last few turns, and he tamped down his amusement.

"You'll see."

Whatever happened, she reacted strongly. If she shut down, it was with ten locked doors and a No Entrance sign blazing. If she let someone in, it was like seeing the sun up close and not getting burned. He liked her highs and lows. Her passionate opinions. He even liked the driven side of her that made her want to leave here—and him—and work somewhere else.

Hunter might not know what was going to happen between them, but in the last few days, he'd been drowning, forgetting that God's imagination was far greater than his. He would choose to have faith that God had a plan. That He loved Hunter and Rachel, and wanted good for them. Yes, Hunter would likely have to give her up all over again. And God's plan might turn out to be different than the one he would come up with, but he was still going to believe and pray and hope even if he didn't know what the future looked like. One day at a time. He could handle that, couldn't he?

He pulled into his friend's driveway, the fading evening light disrupted as his headlights splashed against the front windows of the house.

Hunter unbuckled and hopped out of the truck, met by the Texas heat that reached down his throat and closed like a fist. Rachel stayed in the passenger seat with the belt still on. "Are we going to visit your friends or something? Because I'm not looking my best." She motioned to her workout clothes.

"Nope, we're not. And you look perfect."

She rolled her eyes, and he fought a grin with everything in him. Hunter didn't need a Rachel-induced black eye any time soon.

"Come on."

Her hands tightened on the seat belt that still stretched across her chest, as though holding on would keep her from being ejected from the truck.

"Do I need to come over there and get you?"

She unbuckled lightning fast, the belt clinking against the metal doorframe as she got out.

When she reached his side of the vehicle, he swung the door shut and started walking. Rachel didn't follow, so he went back, grabbed her hand and tugged her along. Stubborn. Two could play at that game. Hunter didn't let go of her hand. If he only got to have her for another week, he might as well enjoy it. Touching her messed with him in ways a whole day in the hot sun without a drop of hydration didn't compare to. Surprisingly, she didn't fight to get away.

He went around the side of the house and found the wooden gate to the backyard, letting go of her hand in order to retrieve the key from under the rock to the right of the path. After popping the lock open, he ushered Rachel into the backyard.

Searching along the wall of the house, he found a light switch. The space sprang to life, a string of outdoor lights stretching from one end of the cement patio area to the other, swooping down and illuminating the pool. Clear, crisp inviting water beckoned.

"No way." Her tone brooked no argument, but Hunter toed off one boot then the other, stuffing his socks inside, while Rachel's voice grew louder. "Hunter McDermott, I am not getting in that pool. Are these people even home? Do they know you're here? Are you breaking and entering?" Her pitch increased to squeaking, breaking-glass level as he knelt and began untying the laces of one of her shoes. It must have taken her a second to process his actions, because he got it and her sock off before she started screeching and generally being feisty, trying to keep the second one out of his reach. For that shoe, he had to wrap an arm around her legs to hold her still and work quickly. But he managed to remove it and her sock, tossing them to the side.

When he stood and faced her, she looked like a mama hen whose babies had been attacked.

He made one last attempt to convince her, nodding toward the water. "You can't deny the appeal. It's two hundred degrees out."

"We wouldn't be alive if it was two hundred degrees out."

"It will feel amazing."

"No." Her ponytail swung back and forth with her head.

"In answer to your earlier question, this is my friend Marc's house. They're out of town. Don't worry, I checked with him. That's who I was texting before we left."

"Great." Sarcasm dripped from the word. "I'm still not going in that pool."

"Okay." His arms relaxed by his sides. "You don't have to."

Her forehead puckered with doubt. "Really?"

"No, not really." She was standing near the edge of the pool—not her smartest choice—and he lunged, taking her out with something near a tackle and catapulting the two of them into the water. Rachel screamed so much on the way in he hoped she remembered to close her mouth.

She came up sputtering and splashing, and he grabbed her hands, holding them still. "Tell me that doesn't feel good."

"It doesn't feel good." At her rote answer, he dunked her. What else was he supposed to do? She was as stubborn as the day was hot. She surfaced fighting and lunged onto his back, trying to take him under. It didn't work.

At his laughter, she whacked him on the back and let go, swimming around to face him. "You're annoying."

"Thank you."

She huffed. "I'm sure my mascara is running everywhere."

He eased closer to her and slid his thumbs under her eyes, swiping away the black and washing the remnants on his fingers into the water. "There." He did it one more time. "You're fine now. Gorgeous as always."

Another eye roll. Would she ever believe him?

Rachel dipped her head back into the water and then stretched her neck from side to side. Letting go. Finally.

Now to get her talking.

"This job…how badly do you want it on a scale of one to ten?"

"Ten."

Ouch. Not even an iota of doubt or wanting to stay.

Her hands played with the water, creating miniature waves. "When I left here the first time, I had something to prove. I think I still do. But that's not the only reason. I've been praying about this, and I don't think God would have opened this door if I wasn't supposed to walk through it."

How could he argue with that?

Her head tilted. "Can I ask you a question?"

"No."

She splashed him and he scrubbed the water from his face with a grin.

"Did you ever date anyone over the years since I've been gone? I mean, I'm sure you did. But anything serious?"

Hello, loaded question. His chest heaved. He couldn't blame her for being curious. He'd asked her as much when she'd first come back and she'd answered him.

"Yes, I dated, but only one serious relationship."

"What happened?"

She wasn't you. And that's when he finally understood why that relationship hadn't worked out, why things—at least on his end—had fizzled. Nadine had been amazing. She'd had a young daughter, and Hunter had liked both of them, but love had stayed out of his reach. He'd broken up with her after he couldn't find a way for his feelings to grow, but he'd never grasped why until now.

"She wasn't the one." His answer hung in the air, snapping like an electrical wire above the pool, threatening to break and fall and electrocute them both.

"Hunter." Her voice was soft, almost mournful, causing his pulse to thrum sluggishly. "I want you to be happy. I hope you find the right one."

He fought to keep from saying something he shouldn't, to bury the emotion coursing through him. "I'm sure she's out there somewhere, crying in her soup because she hasn't found me yet." He opted for humor, and her bark of laughter warmed him.

"I'm sure she is." Now she sounded serious.

Rachel needed to stop being so nice. It was confusing, and he was going to kiss her again if she kept it up.

"I hope you find happiness, too." And he meant it. He'd just prefer if it was with him.

"Thanks." Her eyes crinkled at the corners, the light lashes casting shadows over her cheekbones.

"Can I ask you a question?"

"No."

Her answer mimicked his from earlier, and he chuckled. No one was as quick with a retort as Rachel. He splashed a light amount of water toward her, then continued despite her response. "Are you going to tell me what had you so upset earlier when you came over?"

"What do you mean? I was fine."

Her favorite claim. "Rach, I know you better than that."

He held on to her gaze with his and waited.

"It was just…" Her slight shrug made ripples in the

water. "I told you about getting the job and you just took off. And then I didn't hear from you." She sank lower in the pool, the jut of her chin dipping below the surface. "I didn't know if you were upset or if something was wrong."

She'd missed him. The knowledge rose up, shouting for attention.

"I just had a lot to do with work." *And I was figuring out what to do next about you. About the fact that I can't seem to want anyone but you, you stubborn, gorgeous, annoying woman who's leaving me. Again.*

The fact that she cared, that she'd missed him, was messing with every resolve he'd set to keep himself from doing something stupid—like easing forward to taste her lips again, or to say, *Hey, what if you stayed? How about that?* Just like the last time.

But he wouldn't ask. He couldn't. What had she told him? A ten. That's how badly she wanted this job. And he wasn't going to be the one to stop her.

The irony choked him. After all of these years, he was getting to her. She was opening up again. And now she was moving for sure.

They only had a small amount of time left together, and Hunter planned to spend every minute he could with her. Even knowing his heart was going to just shrivel and give up beating when she left.

She might as well take it with her when she went. He wouldn't have any need for it after she was gone.

"So you weren't upset that I took the job?"

Rachel wasn't sure why she cared so much. Or why she'd sought out Hunter in the first place. But now that they were knee-deep in this conversation, she wanted to finish it. To know.

"No." Some emotion she couldn't decipher flickered in his eyes. "I'm happy for you, Rach. I'm sorry I was MIA."

"It's okay. I don't know what came over me. I think..." The air in her lungs rushed out. "The thought of leaving has me pretty messed up."

"That's understandable. This is your home. It might not be easy to go." Hunter swallowed, his Adam's apple bobbing. "But that doesn't mean it's not the right thing for you."

Peace trickled in. "That's true." Her shoulders inched lower. "Thank you for talking this out with me."

"And for forcing you into the pool."

"No." She wrung her ponytail out. "Not for forcing me into the pool."

Except...maybe a little. Only Hunter could break through her defenses like this. He'd been her best friend when they were younger, and he was dangerously close to owning the position again. Though she hadn't said it, leaving him might be harder than saying goodbye to her nephews. How could she think such a thing? She could get arrested and thrown in aunt jail for a confession like that.

Rachel was losing the battle to stay detached. Who was she kidding? That ship had sailed weeks ago.

But now was not the time to be falling for Hunter again. *Pull yourself together, Maddox.* Her pathetic little pep talk didn't make a dent in her current frame of mind.

The noise of the gate opening made Rachel's head

whip in that direction. A police officer walked into the backyard, his flashlight—and thankfully nothing else—drawn and pointed at them.

"You kids need to get out of there. Trespassing is breaking the law."

Kids? Trespassing? She faced Hunter. Her concern was echoed in the pinch of his brow.

"We're not trespassing," he replied. "I can explain."

The flashlight settled on Hunter's chin. "Do you own this house?"

"No, sir, but my—"

"Then you can explain once you're out of the pool."

Rachel scowled at Hunter, lowering her voice. "I thought you said you had permission to be here?"

"I do. We'll get it straightened out. Don't worry."

Don't worry? Unfortunately she'd ridden in the back of a police car once before, and she had no desire to repeat the experience because Hunter had had a crazy idea.

Once she reached the tiled edge of the pool, Rachel lifted herself out, then followed the police officer and Hunter to the front of the house. Her apprehension lessened at the realization that he didn't have his emergency lights on. And that he made no motion to retrieve the handcuffs hanging from his belt, their metal gleaming in the headlights of the cruiser.

But he did open the back door of the police car. "Get in while we figure this out."

Rachel balked. She'd rather bare her innermost secrets to a group of nosy busybodies than get in that vehicle. But what was she supposed to do? Argue with the officer?

Hunter's hand slipped around hers and squeezed. Warm. Reassuring. "We'll work this out, but we don't need to make him upset." His voice registered just above a whisper, as calm as if they were deciding on which brand of cereal to purchase. "Just get in. It's okay."

But it wasn't. After one long exhale, she ducked and slid into the seat, and Hunter quickly followed.

When the officer asked them why they'd been in the pool when the homeowner wasn't home, Hunter explained. He got out his phone and relayed Marc's number to the officer so he could clear things up. Then they waited.

The air-conditioning in the police car was blasting. Rachel's hair was dripping, her clothes were soaked, her feet bare. She shivered.

Without invitation, Hunter wrapped an arm around her and tucked her against him. When she resisted, he cocked his head back far enough to meet her gaze. "Really? I know you're freezing. I can feel you shaking."

"I'm not." Her chattering teeth gave her away. Fine. She would soak up a little of his warmth. Rachel eased against him, his heat seeping through their wet clothes. She would stay here, crushed against his rock-hard chest, but she wouldn't enjoy it. Not one bit.

"This is a big deal, you know." Once again, she'd just backtracked miles in changing how people thought of her.

Hunter's hand slid up and down her arm. She was not going to admit it felt comforting. Was. Not. "It's not like Marc's going to press charges. They're going to figure out that I know him and that we weren't trespassing."

She ground her jaw tight. "And in the meantime, here

we are, sitting in the back of a cop car. It's like the old Rachel's back."

Again Hunter shifted so he could see her face. "The old Rachel isn't back, but so what if she is? I liked that Rachel. I like this Rachel. You're one and the same."

"I'm not." She certainly hoped she wasn't.

"Why don't you want to be that girl?"

Wasn't it obvious? "She was a screwup." With pretty much everything—life, school, family. Picking the worst guys. "I've worked so hard not to be her anymore."

"You're nowhere near a screwup. I'm not sure why you're so hard on yourself. We didn't do anything wrong tonight. And as for when you were a teenager, so what if you did a few things you regret? There's grace for that. No one thinks anything bad about you."

"The whole town does."

"Rach," he held her gaze, a seriousness unusual for him pulling on his features. "I think that might be in your head. I don't notice anyone treating you that way."

Had she really changed enough to convince everyone? Or had she only imagined they thought the worst of her when it wasn't necessarily true?

"People love you exactly as you are. You were great when you were a teenager and you're just as amazing now. And you're going to be really good at this job." Hunter squared his shoulders. "You're meant for this." His deep breath was audible, his tone somehow conveying pain and sweetness at the same time. "I'm proud of you."

She believed him, but she didn't know why the words hurt. Her emotions felt as though they'd been sent through a blender tonight.

But Hunter was right. They'd get this cleared up. It would work out.

She just didn't have any confidence she could say the same for the state of her falling heart.

Chapter Thirteen

"Whatever you do, don't fall off the float. And don't have any fun."

Hunter's directions caused the teens to laugh and Rachel to do the usual regarding his teasing—shake her head and fight the curve of her lips. It was the morning of the Independence Day parade, and the kids were jittery with excitement. One of them falling off probably wasn't as much of a joke as Hunter made it out to be.

Rachel and Hunter had only spent about twenty minutes in the back of the cop car on Monday before things had worked out exactly like Hunter had said they would. Turned out a neighbor had heard Rachel screaming when Hunter sent her flying into the pool. They'd known Marc was out of town and had thought some kids had broken into the backyard for a swim. But after talking to Marc, the police officer had let them go without issue.

She'd almost forgiven Hunter for the ordeal—not that she planned to admit that to him yet.

Rachel finished applying thick black lines across Bree's cheekbones. A few of the girls had decided to dress as football players. There were other sports represented, too—volleyball, cheerleading, soccer.

At least the float had become about more than just football, but barely.

"Thanks." Bree's gratitude was short and not necessarily sweet. Since she'd overheard Rachel on the phone, she'd shuttered again. Not as badly as the first time around—she was still cordial. Polite. None of the angst from when they'd first met. But she definitely hadn't texted to request another chat on Rachel's swing. When Rachel had asked her about whether she'd talked to her parents, Bree had answered with, "Yep." She hadn't expounded on how the conversation had gone or if she felt any peace. The girl had closed down like a Chickfil-A on Sunday.

Rachel hated that she was hurting Bree, but she wasn't sure what to do about it. Not like she could stay here just for the teen. She wasn't even letting herself consider that option in regard to her family. Or Hunter.

That thought—it was off-limits. She'd already made her decision. No going back now.

With her stuff mostly packed and her departure scheduled for the day after tomorrow, a big boulder had settled in her stomach. It was trying to drag her down, to drown her in doubts over her decision and sorrow over leaving everyone.

The whole lot of them were messing with her dreams of this job in Houston.

But she wasn't going to concentrate on any of that today. Because the day of the parade was finally here. It started in exactly twelve minutes, and Rachel only wanted to think about how hard the kids had worked and how great the float looked. Today was about celebrating their teamwork and even this town that had won over her affections.

Once all of the kids were stationed on the float and had the bags of candy they'd be doling out, she and Hunter climbed into the cab of his truck in order to pull the trailer.

He checked his rear and side view mirrors. The man might joke around. A lot. But she had every confidence he'd keep the kids safe.

"You ready for this?" His face softened as he glanced at her. He made her stomach do backflips and forward flips and cliff dives. Those dimples. She'd probably devoted a page or twenty in her diary to them when she was younger and hadn't wanted to admit to anyone that she thought the neighbor boy was cute. And...it had only taken her one second to veer off course. *We're not going there, today. Remember?*

She managed to nod in answer to his question. About time, too, because he was shooting her a look of concern/confusion.

"They did a great job."

"They did." The same innocent look of contentment Grayson wore when he found a new bug or when Cash took him out on the ranch was evident on Hunter's face, making Rachel pull her resolve tight around her. Two more days and she'd be gone—on to the next step in her life—and she wouldn't have to work at resisting her feelings for Hunter anymore.

She could do it, couldn't she?

She had to. Because if anything more happened between them now, it would only make leaving worse. And she didn't want to do that to either of them.

* * *

They'd survived the parade route without losing any kids and without any injuries, but Hunter was dangerously close to losing his mind. He'd dropped Rachel and the kids off near the festivities so he could drive the float home and leave it in the barn before heading back to town, but the scent of her still lingered in the cab of his truck. Sweet. Torturous.

He was afraid if he failed to stay away from her and she still left, he might just shut down and stop functioning. That would really make Dad mad, having to handle everything on his own without Hunter's help. Perversely, that thought cheered him. Deep down, he did love his father. He just didn't always understand him.

After unhitching the float, Hunter drove back into the packed town. Part of Main Street was still blocked off, and vendors dotted the blacktop, their colorful food trucks and tarped stands boasting homemade goods, American flags and festive trinkets.

He cracked his window and live music drifted in along with a rush of hot air. There'd been a slew of small local bands playing music all day, and they'd continue after dinner so people could dance the night away.

After searching for a spot nearby, Hunter gave up and parked blocks away, hoofing it to the area with long picnic tables spread between booths of food. He scanned for a familiar face and spotted Rachel sitting with her brother, Olivia and the boys. He made his way in their direction. When he neared, she looked up, and her smile lit with her greeting. All of that sunshine, just for him. She was going to kill him with it. Did she have any idea he'd fallen for her all over again? Or that he'd never really stopped?

Hunter shook off the melancholy that attempted to choke him. No pouting. This wasn't a sulking kind of night.

"I got you a plate." She motioned to the seat next to her and a paper plate covered by a napkin. Under it, he found a barbeque sandwich, the local sauce dripping from the meat. Chips were overflowing alongside.

He greeted Cash and Olivia, said hello to the boys then dug in.

They attempted adult conversation—the ranch with Cash and the upcoming volleyball season with Olivia. But the boys were too excited to do anything close to sitting still. They were keyed up, likely spinning from the large amounts of candy that had been tossed to the crowd during the parade. Cash and Olivia did their best to corral them into eating, but Hunter doubted more than a few bites were shoveled in between questions from Grayson.

How late do I get to stay up?

When are the fireworks?

And Hunter's personal favorite—*When can we get dessert?*

Ryder toddled along the seat, and Grayson climbed up on the picnic bench, then got down numerous times until Cash finally gave an exasperated sigh and stood. He swung Ryder onto his shoulders and reached for Grayson's hand. "Let's go pick out a piece of pie."

At Grayson's cheer and Ryder's clapping approval, Olivia stood and joined them. "We'll be back."

Rachel waved as they walked away, then faced Hunter. Tears glistened in her eyes.

"You okay?"

Her head bobbed but then changed directions. "No." She blinked back the moisture. "How am I going to leave them?"

It was painful not to plead his case. They all had reasons for wanting her to stay. Hunter was confident Cash and Olivia wanted her to live here just as much as he did. But they all quietly knew the same thing—the choice had to be hers. No one was going to impose an opinion on her. "You're going to be amazing. And you'll be back to visit."

Her eyelids closed and she nodded again. "You're right."

"Kind of prideful, if you ask me." At his teasing, her eyes popped open and she laughed. The sound made him happy and sad all at the same time.

"I meant the part about coming back to visit."

"I know." Hunter had cleared his plateful of barbeque in record time and now, much like Grayson, he couldn't wait for dessert. He pushed up from the bench, motioning for her to join him. "Let's go get something sweet." Hunter would gladly forgo sugar of the baking variety and choose Rachel instead, but unfortunately, that option wasn't on the menu.

She stood, her flowered sundress flirting above her knees as they gathered their trash.

By the time they'd stood in line and then finished their pieces of fresh strawberry pie, the band had switched and a new one had started. Kids were spread across a corner of the dance floor, shaking out their excess energy with crazy dance moves while the adults two-stepped. Cash and Liv were dancing, Ryder held between them while Grayson looked like he'd been two-stepping since he was born. He'd even asked a little girl to dance. A bit choppy, but still, impressive.

Rachel tracked him, her face glowing with pride and amusement. "I'm afraid he's starting young."

"Some of us do."

They stood next to each other, watching everyone spin past them for two more songs while a war raged within him. Should he ask her to dance? Did that qualify in the friend category? Or would she sense everything he wasn't telling her? And would Rachel even say yes?

He felt like a teenager again—minus the awkward voice cracking, thank the good Lord above.

When the smooth notes of George Strait's "The Chair" began, Hunter decided to man up and stop being a wuss.

"Seems like a waste to listen to all of this music and not dance to at least one song."

"It does seem like a waste." Rachel peered around him, straining to see who knew what. "I wonder who might be willing to dance with you, McDermott. I saw Patty Holster over by the popcorn stand." Patty was sweet all right. And she'd had white hair for as long as he'd been alive. Kind of like he assumed Rachel had been sassy since birth. "I think she'd love to—"

He interrupted her by pulling her onto the floor, and her words were swallowed up by laughter. Asking was overrated. In typical Rachel style, she completely baffled him by easing into his arms without complaint—almost as though she'd been waiting for that very thing. The woman was all things confusing, and he couldn't get enough of her. He wasn't sure what that said about him.

After a few times around, she let go of a sigh that

could only mean contentment. Her shoulders relaxed and her eyes closed as though savoring a bite of her favorite dessert.

She was going to be the death of him. And he no longer cared to fight it.

It was time for fireworks, and everyone was camped out on their blankets or chairs, looking for the best spot to catch every pop of color.

Rachel had helped Gray find a bathroom, and now she watched him scoot through the pockets of people until he reached his mom, dad and Ryder. He plopped into Olivia's lap, making everyone laugh. Liv said something in Cash's ear, and he kissed the top of her head. Sappy as always. Once the two of them had figured out they were perfect for each other, they'd been the kind of steady a person could use for a building foundation.

It wasn't the first time Rachel wished her parents could have met Liv. They would have loved her as much as Cash did. As much as Rachel did. The ache of missing her parents spread through her. She wanted her mom. Wanted to talk to her about Hunter. About the job. About everything.

Rachel could go for some wisdom right now.

Instead of going to sit with Cash, Liv and the boys, she leaned back against the building behind her. She'd let them enjoy this time as a family. They looked so peaceful, so right together. Would she ever have that? Or was she leaving that behind when she went to Houston on Monday?

Hunter appeared, settling beside her in comfortable silence. If Rachel let herself daydream, she could imagine herself married to the man next to her. They'd go home together after the fireworks. She'd live in this town she'd thought she hated, and she'd be content. Happy.

But would she? Despite her growing feelings for Hunter, she still wanted the job in Houston. She'd worked so hard for it. She couldn't just let it go now.

The fireworks started, the booming noise causing more than a few kiddos to cover their ears. Bits of red and white shot through the sky, dripping like spilled paint until it looked as though the sparks would stay lit all the way to the ground.

Rachel kept her gaze forward as long as she could. When she couldn't resist any longer, she glanced at Hunter. He wasn't looking at the fireworks. He was watching her.

The uneven thumping in her chest increased as she glued her eyes back on the sparkling sky.

Trouble. She'd called him the word more times than she could count. But now she was beginning to think she'd underestimated the kind of havoc he would wreak on her heart when she left.

After a few more minutes, the *pop-pop-pop* of the finale rang out as blue, green, white and red flashes of color all fought for space against the charcoal sky. A hint of smoke hung in the air after the last blast, and the crowd cheered before quickly starting to disperse.

She and Hunter were as close as they could be without physically touching. He had picked her up this morning for the parade, but it would make sense for her to catch a ride home with Cash and Liv. They'd drive right by her place.

Rachel could avoid the sensation flowing between

herself and Hunter. She could skip out on the turmoil this time around.

He nudged her shoulder with his. "Am I dropping you off?"

Yes. Her desires momentarily outweighed her maturity.

"I'll ride with Cash and Liv. There's no reason for you to drive past your ranch."

His lips pressed together. Finally, he agreed. "Probably a good idea. Let's find them, then."

They tried to ease into the crowd, but a stroller cut Rachel off, and she waited for it to pass. Hunter had paused to wait for her, and when she caught up, he snagged her hand and started walking again. He had a habit of doing that—always without permission—and she told herself it didn't mean anything. Usually he just wanted to direct her somewhere she didn't want to go, and it was his way of getting her there.

Tonight, he was simply making sure they stuck together in the crowd. But it didn't feel simple. And all of the other times he'd touched her or clasped her hand hadn't, either. His skin was warm and calloused—who knew she'd ever consider that an attractive quality?—and right at home against hers.

Somehow she needed to silence the teenager inside of her who clamored for one more kiss. The one who wanted to pretend she wasn't moving.

Who didn't care how much she got hurt.

If ever there was a night for Rachel to be mature, to cling to her last thread of dignity, this was it.

They caught up to Cash and Liv. Her brother had one hand linked with Grayson's, the other full of blankets and supplies. Liv held Ryder, who looked sleepy despite the recent noise level.

Cash greeted them. "You riding with us, Rach?"

"Yep." She turned to Hunter. "Thanks. I'll see you… tomorrow? At church?"

His head hitched in response, and then he was gone, disappearing with long strides into the crowd. Rachel took the blanket and diaper backpack from her brother. He scooped Gray onto his shoulders, and the four of them made their way to the car.

The whole walk, the whole ride home, Rachel told herself she'd made the right choice. Saying no to Hunter's offer to drive her was the smart thing to do. What would be the point of starting something now? It would never work between them. She was moving to a job she wanted in a town that offered so much more than this one, and she still had something to prove—if not to the people here, then to herself. And Hunter would always live here. His whole life revolved around ranching.

Even if the organ in her chest was barely beating from all of the abuse, she'd made the right choice.

It took Hunter forever and a day to get to his truck, and by then, the traffic was at a standstill. Now he was almost home. Finally.

He'd managed, somehow, to keep from kissing Rachel today. From telling her how he felt about her. But he was hanging by a thread. Hunter had no idea how he would survive tomorrow night at the going-away dinner Cash and Olivia were hosting. Or saying goodbye to Rachel on Monday morning.

No clue.

Loving her was a fire he couldn't extinguish. And he didn't want to—even if she was going to leave him.

It was a good thing Rachel had gone home with her brother. Hunter didn't have any resolve left when it came to her. Overnight, he'd shore up again.

Somehow.

He pulled up to his house, concern slithering through him at the sight of Rachel's Jeep. Was something wrong? He turned off the truck and got out, slamming the door. The sound reverberated in the otherwise quiet night.

Rachel had been sitting on his front steps, and now she stood. Her feet were bare, the strappy heeled sandals she'd worn earlier retired for the evening or, knowing her, left on the floor of the Jeep. She still had on the sundress that had messed with his mind all day. She looked gorgeous in it. But then, she looked amazing in anything.

With every step she took toward him, he fought two emotions—need and fear.

Once she reached him, she paused, mere inches separating him from everything he wanted and couldn't have.

The shyest look crossed her face. As if she'd come all this way and now couldn't say what she needed to.

"You okay?"

She nodded. "I just…" She shrugged in a helpless gesture, lips pressed together as if stemming her next words.

Before he could think, his hands were on her shoulders. Their gazes melded, tenderness passing between them. "Rach, tell me you don't want me to kiss you."

"I don't want you to kiss me." Not one part of him trusted her response.

For the first time all day, he let his guard down. "I don't believe you."

Her mouth barely had time to reach for a smile before his lips met hers. The pain of knowing he was losing her again wrapped into their kiss, and time and space stood still.

Her lips were sweet and soft, and he was afraid he'd never let her go.

Easing back, he rested his forehead against hers.

"This is a stupid idea."

Her face broke into the kind of smile that held a secret. That could light up the night sky with electricity. "I know. It's idiotic. I'm sorry I came over."

"I'm not."

At his answer, he saw something in her shift. Soften. She propped her bare feet on the top of his boots, wrapped her arms around his neck and held on. He squeezed her close, nose buried in her fragrant hair.

When their lips met again, there was no hesitation in her kiss. She was all his, even if it was only for a moment.

He'd never loved her more.

Chapter Fourteen

"**G**ive me that." Val snatched the veggie tray from Rachel's hand. "This is your going-away party. You're not supposed to be helping."

It wasn't exactly a party. More of a dinner. Olivia and Cash were hosting, and Lucy and Graham were in attendance along with their girls, Val and Brennon and Connor, plus Hunter. It was a madhouse, but it was the best possible kind. Rachel had spent most of the evening trying not to cry. She'd gotten everything she'd worked for, so why was this so hard? It was nothing like the last time she'd left. Colorado had been so far. Now she'd be much closer—a four-hour drive away. She could come back for a weekend easily.

But that wasn't making her feel better.

She was moving tomorrow, and last night she'd been kissing Hunter like she never planned to leave.

"What's going on?" Val set the tray on the table, studying Rachel much like she'd done with her chemistry homework in high school while the two of them were supposed to be working and Rachel had done anything but. They'd been friends long enough that Rachel knew better than to try to hide from her.

"I'm moving."

"Uh-huh. We've known that for a while. Tell me what's changed."

"Hunter."

People filled the first floor of the house, but between the loud conversations and wild kids, Rachel felt confident no one would overhear their hushed conversation in the corner near the dining room table.

"Oh." Her friend's face held a hint of amused *I knew it* with a side of concern. "He pulled you in, did he?"

Moisture pooled in Rachel's eyes. "It hurts that I'm moving away. I'm going to miss all of you."

"But especially him." Val's tone held no malice. "Do you…have you thought about the job? Do you still—"

"Want it?" Rachel's voice escalated with panic, and she dialed her volume back to a two. "Yes, I do." She was a mess. She'd never been so torn about anything in all of her life. Except maybe the last time she'd left. This ranked right up close to that experience. "What is wrong with me that I still do?"

"Nothing." Val's loose brown curls shook, her tone brooking no argument. "There's nothing wrong with you or your aspirations. I'm guessing you want to stay with him, too."

Fingers seeking the familiar comfort of her gold R necklace, Rachel slid the pendant back and forth on the chain. "It scares me, but I think so." Her mind spun at the truth she'd been avoiding. "But what can I do about that? How's that going to work? Part of me wonders if I'll ever forgive myself for giving Hunter up again. I've never felt about anyone the way I do about him. I told him we shouldn't get involved. I tried to stay away. To keep my distance." She paused and waited for Grayson and Lola to swing around the table and grab handfuls of pretzels before quietly continuing. "But it didn't work. Now what do I do?"

Compassion radiated from Val. "Oh, honey. I think you need to talk to him."

"But I don't want to," Rachel wailed with a childish flair, making them laugh, though hers was mournful. "I'm not sure what he's thinking, and I'm afraid to find out." Did he care about her as more than a friend? Was what they had real? Or just a mistake?

"The two of you didn't discuss any of this after your smoochy-smoochy last night?" Val made a tsking sound. "Kids these days."

"You and I are the same age!" Despite her misery, Rachel laughed. "And to answer your question, no we didn't. I just…left. I wasn't sure what to say. If it was just a goodbye, I'll always care about you kind of moment or something more. I needed time to process. But I'm realizing that I'm not okay with losing him again."

"Talk. To. Him." Huh. Val's counsel sounded strangely similar to what Rachel had advised Bree to do. But it was a whole lot easier to dole out than to follow.

"And say what?"

Baby Senna gave a disgruntled cry, and the voices in the room quieted for a second. Val waited, then continued once the hum of other conversations resumed. "Only you know the answer to that."

"I want it all." The selfish truth rolled from her tongue. "The job and him."

"Then tell him that."

"I can't. How will that help anything? How would that scenario ever work?"

"You'll be four hours away. Not impossible that you could date long-distance."

Rachel had thought about that option during her restless night. But to what end? Hunter belonged here—and although this life had grown on her over the summer and she was going to miss it, she still wasn't sure it was a fit for her. If she didn't go to Houston, she'd always wonder. She'd never know for sure.

Either way, Val was right. Rachel had to hash this out with him.

She grabbed a brownie from the table and took a bite, letting the sweet cocoa do its best to ease her tension. What would she do without Val in her life? They'd been friends a long time. Val knew all of her worst parts and loved her, anyway. She was the sweet to Rachel's sass. The two of them had always made a good team.

"I'm not sure you deserve the credit for that solution. Technically, I came up with what I need to say. You just listened while I processed."

"Whatever." Val tossed a baby carrot at Rachel. It bounced off the top portion of her black maxi dress and landed on the floor, making them giggle like they had so often back in their younger days. "Even counselors need a listening ear *and* some advice once in a while." Her friend's smile turned down at the edges, sadness seeping in. "And in case you're wondering, I'm going to miss you, too."

"Did you get two pieces of cake?"

Grayson stood before Hunter, hands on his hips.

He looked far more foreboding than any four-year-old should.

Hunter wasn't sure whether to tell him the truth or fudge, so he went for evasive. "Did you?"

"No. Mama said I couldn't have more than one. She said the sugars make me hyper." His nose wrinkled. "I don't know what that means but I don't like it."

"That's rough."

"I wanted Auntie Rachel to get a bug cake, so she picked a ladybug one for me. Still girly, but at least she tried."

"That was nice of her."

"Yup. Auntie Rach is the best."

Hunter agreed.

"Hey, are you two talking about me?" Rachel came from behind Hunter, joining the two of them.

He winked at Grayson. "We were discussing guy stuff."

The boy's mouth curved. "You wouldn't understand, Auntie Rachel."

She scoffed, then grabbed him up in a hug while he squealed and squirmed. "Hey, your mom says it's time for bed. Story time? It's our last night."

Rachel looked as though she was fighting back emotion. Grayson nodded, not seeming to notice his aunt's upset, and the two of them took off upstairs.

Cash was putting Ryder down, and Olivia had walked the other guests outside a few minutes ago. The front window framed the group still talking by their vehicles. Hunter had picked up Rachel on his way over, so he made himself useful and started clearing the table while he waited for her.

He'd just deposited a platter of veggies in the fridge when Olivia came back in.

"Hunter, you really don't need to do that."

"I don't mind." She took him at his word, which he appreciated, and the two of them worked quickly. By the time he heard Rachel's footsteps on the stairs, they'd made a huge dent in the cleanup.

"Gray's down. I'm not sure if he'll sleep, though. He's all ramped up from running around with the kids. Cash is going to try reading him one more book to see if it helps."

"Thank you." Olivia waved a hand. "He'll settle down eventually."

"What can I do?" Rachel came into the kitchen where they were working.

"Nothing. It's almost done thanks to Hunter."

"I don't deserve all of the credit." In fact, he'd rather have none of it.

Olivia smiled in answer and turned to Rachel. "I'm sure you have more to pack. Why don't you two head out?"

"I can help." Her voice wobbled, and in response, Olivia's eyes filled with tears.

Oh, boy. Hunter glanced around for an escape but didn't see any rocks he could crawl under. He needed to drive Rachel home, so he couldn't bolt before the waterworks started.

Olivia swiped under her lashes. "We are not doing this tonight. Hunter, get her out of here, already. She's going to turn me into a bumbling mess."

When he didn't move fast enough, Olivia raised an eyebrow at him as if questioning his snail-like pace.

Hunter wasn't one to make a woman upset if at all possible, so he obeyed.

"Yes, ma'am." He approached Rachel like he might a skittish barn cat. "Come on, let's get you home."

In response, she crossed her arms. "No. I'm going to help clean up."

Both women looked like their decision had been chiseled in stone, which left Hunter stuck in the middle. One had fed him, the other he loved. He went with the one who'd fed him, partly because it seemed like the right thing to do. Partly because he liked getting a rise out of Rachel.

Relying on his old standby, he bent and scooped Rachel up at the knees, swinging her over his shoulder. She whacked him on the back, complaining loudly. Something about a caveman. About how he couldn't just manhandle her all of the time. But of course he already was, so she'd pretty much lost that argument.

Olivia had a goofy smile on her face, and Hunter wasn't sure what that meant, so he thanked her for dinner and then swung Rachel around so that she faced her sister-in-law. Upside down and backward, but it worked.

Rachel thanked Olivia for hosting and then complained that she wasn't helping her escape from Hunter. After her upset earned a laugh from Olivia instead of assistance, Hunter headed for his truck.

He managed to make it through the door without bonking Rachel's head on the frame, and when he got to his truck, he set her down by the passenger side. Her hair was mussed from being upside-down, but it fell in beautiful disarray. Her back was to the vehicle, and his hands landed on either side of her. She still had tears glistening in her gorgeous green eyes.

Killing. Him.

"Rach, it's going to be okay." His hands slid to her face, cradling. "It's going to be okay."

He wasn't sure if he was repeating it for himself or for her. Maybe both.

"How do you know?"

"I just do." And he did. Hunter had been praying nonstop in the last week, and despite all of the turmoil he was about to face with Rachel moving, he felt peace. It was palpable, the knowledge that he had *no idea* what was going to happen next, but that God had a plan greater than he could imagine. Hunter was clinging to that belief.

He leaned forward and pressed his lips to hers. It was an assurance, meant to comfort. At least, that's how it started out. But then Rachel's fingers slid into his hair, pulling him under her current. How could she kiss him like this and not want to stay? He gave up on trying to stay afloat and let himself drown in her touch. If only he could spend the rest of his life doing exactly this. He didn't ask for much, did he?

After a few seconds, Hunter wrenched himself away. Caught his breath. "Rachel Marie Maddox, are you trying to get me seriously injured?"

Her eyes flew wide with innocence. "Why?"

"Your brother is going to come out here with a shot gun in a matter of seconds."

That, of all things, made her smile.

He ripped open her door and ushered her inside. The drive to her house was silent and fraught with tension.

Once they arrived at her place, he put the truck in Park. She reached over, turned the ignition off. "Come on."

He felt like a spider who could see the sticky trap coming, but refused to change courses. Stupid spider.

Still, he didn't resist. Hunter followed her out of the vehicle and up the steps. Moose stretched and stood, nuzzling both of them until he received the rubdown he was looking for. After he was satisfied, he curled back up on the soft rug Rachel had put out for him.

Rachel faced Hunter, her sadness painfully evident.

What was going on? Was it something besides the obvious?

"Rach, talk to me. What is wrong?"

Her hands jutted out, shoving against his chest but not moving him. "I don't want to leave you."

The words held in the air, a lightning strike of electricity. Hunter had to work to breathe in. Out. To not beg her to stay. He'd once promised her he wouldn't ask her to stay again, and he *would* honor that.

"I'm going to miss you." She sniffled.

"I'll miss you, too." There. That was safe. Truthful.

"I don't even know what I'm doing anymore. What I'm thinking. I feel so confused."

Warnings sirens flared to life in his mind.

She couldn't be considering not going, could she? How would that ever work? If it was because of him, she'd always wonder. He wouldn't be enough to hold her here, and then she'd leave, just like his mother.

She had to go. No matter how much he wished the outcome could be different. He knew how important this job was to her. What had she said to him that night?

A ten.

Any feelings she had for him at this point weren't enough. If she wanted to stay beyond a shadow of a doubt—if she picked this life—that would be different.

But she wasn't making that choice. Obviously. Because she was telling him she was going to miss him when she moved. Which meant she was still going.

Tears cascaded down her cheeks, each one inflicting a new stab wound. Hunter could handle just about anything, but Rachel crying might do him in. He'd much rather be the one hurting.

He allowed himself to slide thumbs across her adorable freckles and wipe away the moisture.

"What are we going to do? I don't know how to leave you. Do we try long-distance?"

He hadn't even thought of that. She'd only be four hours away. He could finally tell her how he felt about her. And they might be able to hang on for a little while. Schedule times to see each other. Make the trek back and forth. But eventually the truth would surface: it was never going to work. She wanted that world and he had a life here. Dating long-distance would only prolong the pain for both of them.

"We can't."

Hurt etched across her sweet face. "What do you mean, we can't?"

"We just can't." He couldn't be the person holding her back. How could she not understand that?

She was crumbling right before his eyes. And he was wounding them both. But better now than later. If they dated, he'd always be pulling her back here. They needed a clean break. A chance for Rachel to embrace the life she'd dreamed about without him in the way.

"You don't belong here."

The light in her eyes flickered. He wanted with everything in him to bring it back, but what he'd said was true. She deserved a better life than this. She should live in the city with all the conveniences she wanted. This town wasn't right for her.

He thought of his mom. Of all the days she'd been unable to get out of bed. The dark circles that had resided under her eyes. The number of times she'd turned the other way to hide her tears from him but he'd seen them, anyway. He held on to those memories for all he was worth, the reminder exactly what he needed.

"What did you just say?" Her voice was soft, sorrow seeping into every crevice.

"You don't belong here. You should go."

Hunter knew his words had wounded her by the fresh tears rolling down her cheeks and the way her face crinkled with pain. She'd softened so much since she'd come back. And now he was ruining all of it. He'd never have another chance with her. This was it. The end of so many years of wanting her, even when he hadn't realized his feelings were still there, lying dormant, waiting for a spark of hope to ignite them again.

She shifted closer to him, and he braced himself for a slap. Her hand did land on his cheek, but it was gentle. "I don't believe you."

They were the same words he'd said before kissing her. His eyes shuttered, overcome by her touch, by the last time he'd ever feel it. *Just go. Please, please don't make me do this.* He wasn't sure he had the strength to continue.

"You should believe me. We're not right for each other. I always knew you were moving." The words made what they'd had sound cheap, though it had been anything but. His voice was wooden, yet emotion still sprang behind his eyes. He needed to get out of here before she found out the truth.

He stepped back from her, from that questioning, injured look she now wore, and then, after allowing himself one more long drink of memorizing everything about her, he turned. He flew down the steps and across the drive to his truck as fast as he could, afraid that if he looked back, he'd be holding her in his arms, apologizing, before he could count to one.

He kept walking, even when he heard her sob, even when his heart tore in two.

He wasn't sure he'd ever be put back together again. And that was fine by him. Hunter would rather live with the pain of a thousand lifetimes than have her experience one moment of getting stuck in a life she didn't want.

Chapter Fifteen

The little ranch house looked sad and lonely in Rachel's rearview mirror as she headed down her drive for the last time on Monday morning. No lights left on. No Moose lazing on the porch. Rachel had already made a trip over to Cash and Liv's this morning to drop off the dog. Cash planned to deliver him to the shelter for her later today because she was too tormented to do it herself.

She'd only slept a few minutes last night in between horrid dreams. Most had revolved around her parents and that final fight with her mom. Some had trekked into Hunter land. She'd been crying out to him, but he'd had a hollow look in his eyes. He'd turned and walked away while her sobs had echoed to nothing.

A repeat of last night. Of course she hadn't thrown herself on the ground and engaged in an all-out toddler tantrum in front of Hunter. Rachel could turn off her emotions when needed. It was a skill that had served her well over the years. One she would use today as she said goodbye to Cash, Liv and the boys.

She'd heard nothing from Hunter this morning. He

had planned to come over to see her off with her family. But now she no longer expected to see him.

Rachel couldn't quit turning the conversation with him round and round in her mind. It had been so strange. She'd been confident Hunter felt something for her, like she did for him. But then he'd just pushed her away without giving them a chance to figure things out. And that hurt. So much.

Last night she'd let herself cry. Today, she needed to be numb to get through this last goodbye.

She pulled up to Cash and Liv's. They must have been listening for the sound of her Jeep, because they came out of the house and down the steps just as she turned off the ignition and got out.

Olivia peppered her with motherly questions, making sure Rachel hadn't forgotten any of the necessities she'd need to get by for the next few weeks while she slept on Dana's couch and hunted for an apartment.

Once she found one, Cash would help her move the rest of her stuff down.

Olivia stepped forward and wrapped her in a long hug. "Rach." She pulled away, face wrinkled with concern. "I don't know what's going on or what happened, hon, but I think maybe—"

"I should really get going." Rachel cut her off. It was something the teenage Rachel would have done, and she wasn't proud of it. But, then again, she wasn't as far from that immature girl as she'd like to think. Hadn't she just made another stupid decision in letting herself get attached to Hunter when she'd always planned to move?

Rachel bent to receive a tackle hug from Grayson, keeping her eyes closed so the tears wouldn't escape.

"Who's going to go riding with me, Auntie Rachel?"

She memorized his baby cheeks and soft lashes. How much more grown up would he look the next time she saw him? "Your dad will go with you. And your mom when she can. And I'll come visit." Except…she wasn't exactly in a rush to do that. Rachel was right back to where she'd started. She didn't want to be in this town.

She stood and accepted Ryder from Cash. He gave her a squirmy hug, then laid a palm on her cheek. She almost broke down right then and there. After kissing his pudgy hand, she shoved him into Liv's open arms, afraid she was never going to give him up if she held on a second longer.

Cash stayed facing her as Olivia and the boys walked back to the house. He had that analyzing look on his face—the one that said he didn't believe her. She remembered it well. He'd used it a lot when she was in high school.

"I know you're upset about something. This was supposed to be a good thing, you getting the job. This was what you wanted, right? What's going on with you?"

She concentrated on the house over his shoulder, the snap of the screen door as the boys and Liv went inside. "I'm fine."

"When Liv says something is fine it's never true."

That almost pulled a laugh out of her.

"Is it something with Hunter? I kind of thought the two of you…"

The beginning of a smile crashed from her face, and the flimsy dam she'd built around her emotions shattered. "What? That we'd get married and live on the ranch next to yours? That we'd be one big, happy family? It's not going to happen, Cash. Everyone knew I was leaving. We shouldn't have gotten so involved."

"We?"

Stink. She'd been thinking about Hunter.

"I need to go." Rachel hugged her brother. Her motions were stunted, and she pulled away quickly, needing to escape. Praying he would understand, she made a break for it, hopping into her Jeep. One wave later she was headed down the road. Just her and a whole lake of tears for company. Well, that was just fine. She was better off on her own, anyway. She could take care of herself. Getting involved with people always hurt.

She had once confronted Cash about that very thing with Olivia. He'd needed a little push to take the leap. And she knew he'd never looked back. Never regretted one single day. Rachel had learned that lesson watching him, and she'd been willing to shove past that fear. She'd wanted more with Hunter. She still didn't know what they would have done had he admitted feelings for her, but they would have worked it out.

But now? Now she didn't have to worry about anyone but herself once again. The thought should have brought relief, but it didn't. What had Hunter said last night? She didn't belong here. The words sent a shiver down her spine. She knew that. She didn't belong anywhere. But her stubborn heart hadn't listened to her numerous warnings. She'd begun to hope again. Silly Rachel. Didn't she know better by now?

Rachel would be fine on her own. She didn't need home or family. She had friends—or at least acquaintances. A new career.

She would be fine.

And maybe if she kept telling herself that, one of these days she'd even believe it.

Rachel had been gone six days—seven if he counted today. Hunter wasn't sure he'd managed a coherent conversation since. He'd forced himself to go to church this morning, hoping it would snap him out of the funk he'd fallen into. God hadn't left him yet, but He might be the only one sticking with Hunter.

He kept telling himself he'd done the right thing. Letting Rachel go had been the best thing for her. This way she could follow her dreams without interruption from him.

But he missed her so much it was all he could do to get up every day and keep functioning. All week he'd poured himself into work, hoping it might lessen the sting. He'd tried not to think about her, but that hadn't worked. Autumn had attempted to talk to him, to figure out what was going on, but he'd clammed up like Fort Knox. Or like Rachel.

The sermon had been on trust this morning. Hunter had thought he had a handle on that. But he couldn't shake the niggling thought that somewhere along the way, he'd missed that part of his faith. He believed… but did he really trust? If he had, wouldn't he have told Rachel the truth instead of pushing her away? They could have prayed over their relationship. Figured out what God had planned. His thoughts jumbled. Had he done the wrong thing? Hunter didn't know anymore, but it didn't matter. She would never forgive him for what he'd said, for the way he'd responded to her. And she'd probably never believe him if he did confess how he felt about her. He'd worked hard to gain her trust again, and then he'd thrown it all away.

He spotted Val in front of him in the church narthex, and before he could stop himself, he was touching her arm. Gaining her attention.

"McDermott." Her face held nothing but contempt for him, and he didn't blame her.

"How is she?" Val could be mad at him, but it would be worth it if he could get a little info about Rachel. "Is she okay?"

"No, she's not okay." Her voice snapped like the little white firecrackers kids threw to the ground on the Fourth of July. Strange coming from the usually even-keeled woman in front of him. "Why do you want to know, anyway?" Her eyes narrowed. "Why *do* you want to know? If you're so interested in her well-being, why'd you push her away?"

"She needed…" What could he say without giving everything away? "This was her dream." He cut himself off before he said too much. It might not be enough of an explanation for her, but it was all he had.

Brennon stopped next to his wife, his concerned look jutting between the two of them.

"Everything okay?"

"Yep." Their answers were simultaneous.

"I'm going to run and get Connor from the nursery." Val backed away as if she'd rather be next to a person with an infectious disease right now than him.

She headed for the steps, and Brennon watched her go before turning back to Hunter.

"How's the hole you dug?"

Hunter let out a noise that was half laugh, half disgusted sigh. "Excellent, thanks for asking."

"Listen, I think I have a way you can fix this. I just heard from one of the school board members that the high school is adding another guidance counselor this year. The money just came through, and they only have a few weeks to fill it. This is perfect for Rachel. Call her. Go see her. Convince her to come back. Not to sound selfish about the whole thing, but I'd really like my sweet, happy wife back."

Despite wanting his friend to have exactly that, Hunter wasn't about to do what Brennon said. That would defeat the whole purpose of letting Rachel go in the first place.

"At least tell me you'll think about it. You're a mess. Rachel's a mess. I don't understand what's going on in your head."

And he couldn't. Hunter didn't need Brennon knowing and then telling Val, who would then tell Rachel. Nope. Things had to stay as they were, no matter how much Hunter wanted a different ending. He'd come this far. He wasn't going to change his mind now.

"I'll think about it." Hunter could add that to his list of untruths.

Brennon took off to catch up with Val and Connor, and Hunter headed for the church doors. This time, it was his phone that made him pause.

It was a text from Autumn.

Remember we're celebrating Dad's birthday today with lunch at his house. I've got all of the food. (You're welcome.) So just come. And don't even think about skipping. I just saw you at church so I know where you are and how long it should take you to get there.

Perfect. Hanging with his family ranked nowhere on his want list for the day. Hunter had penciled in moping and kicking things. So much for that.

Could he use checking on Moose as an excuse to skip out on lunch? After Rachel had left, Hunter had headed over to the shelter and adopted him, hoping the pooch would give him something to focus on and lessen the sting of missing Rachel. No offense to Moose, because Hunter did have a soft spot for the big oaf, but the dog wasn't a worthy replacement for his girl.

And since Hunter had left Moose outside with water and food under a big shade tree, that excuse wouldn't fly.

He texted Autumn back.

Fine. I'll be there.

You'd better be.

I already said I'll be there!

Hunter shoved the phone back in his pocket. He was irritable enough to not want to celebrate anything—especially his equally grumpy father—but Autumn would never let him get away with that. He wasn't even sure why she wanted him there today. He wasn't exactly pleasant company.

Fear wound around his throat, choking him. After all he'd done in order not to turn into his father, he was sure acting and sounding a lot like him.

Maybe he already was him.

Scary thought.

Hunter went to lunch. He even ate lasagna, but he

wasn't happy about it. Except for when Kinsley climbed into his lap and tried to push his mouth out of a frown by manipulating his cheeks. He had a soft spot the size of the Grand Canyon for his niece.

At least Autumn waited until Kinsley ran off to play before launching her inquisition.

"What in the world is going on with you?"

The million-dollar question. He'd learned at least one thing about himself in the process of losing Rachel a second time—he was no good at hiding his emotions. After the first breakup, Autumn had known immediately something was wrong. And now? Felt like the whole town knew.

Except for his dad, who barely looked up from his slice of lemon meringue pie.

Autumn's husband, Calvin, was a quiet guy. Steady. Good to Hunter's sister. Not one for conflict, based on the way his eyes widened and scanned the room for an escape.

Hunter empathized.

"I don't understand why you just let Rachel go." Autumn's voice heated, scorching like cement under bare feet on a sizzling summer day. "I heard there's an opening at the high school for a guidance counselor. Are you going to let her know?" How did everyone know about this position but him? And why were they all pushing? Next thing he knew, even his dad would be weighing in.

Calvin stood. "I'll just…clear some dishes."

Hunter considered running for it along with his brother-in-law, but decided to tough it out. He'd have to face Autumn sooner or later. Might as well get it over with.

"I told you in the beginning we were only friends.

That was the plan. Right along with her moving." He was pleasantly surprised by how calm he sounded. Usually composure came easily to him, but it felt like his laid-back nature had hitchhiked a ride out of town with Rachel. He was afraid it might never come back—another thing that eerily reminded him of his father.

"So, no, I'm not going to let Rachel know about the job. She's a big girl. She can make her own decisions."

"Were you two dating?" Dad's gruff interest mystified Hunter, and it must have done the same to Autumn, because both of their gazes swung to him. "What?" He scowled. "Can't I have an interest in my son's life?"

Hunter clenched his jaw to keep from saying any one of the not-so-kind comments filtering through his mind. Since when did Dad care about what went on in their lives? Had Hunter entered some parallel universe? Or maybe he was still dreaming and hadn't woken up for church yet.

"No." His answer to his father's first question came out far more sad than angry. "We weren't."

Autumn attempted to say more, but Hunter switched the conversation to the ranch—despite his sister's glare—and Dad took it from there.

After a bit, Autumn and Calvin rounded up Kinsley to take her home for a nap. Hunter offered to finish cleaning up and sent them off. He made a trip into the kitchen and returned to find his dad still sitting at the table, studying him as though he could predict the next year's weather. A bit unnerving since the man rarely noticed anything about anyone but himself.

"Autumn is right. You should tell Rachel about the job, you know. She might be interested."

Hunter braced his hands on the table. Hung his head.

The pressure of Rachel leaving and everyone having an opinion about it felt like a precariously slippery ditch he couldn't seem to climb out of. Every time he tried, someone shoved him back down.

His dad didn't have a clue what he was talking about. And he needed to leave it alone. "Who are you to have an opinion about my life? You checked out back when mom left, maybe even before that, and you haven't been present since." The words were a landslide he couldn't get back. But part of him didn't want to. It might have come out without thought, but it was true.

Surprisingly, his dad didn't immediately have a retort. He simply released an audible breath, rubbing a hand across his forehead. "I know."

Hunter couldn't believe what he'd just heard. His dad never admitted fault. In business. In his personal life. Never.

"I wasn't there for you. I thought building a business, a ranch for you to take over one day would show you I loved you. I avoided the pain of your mom's troubles by concentrating on work." His dad's eyes filled with moisture—a sight Hunter had only witnessed once in his life. All of these years he'd wondered and hadn't asked. Well, now he was mad enough to let the words flow.

"Why did you do it? Why did you convince Mom to marry you when you knew she didn't want to live on a ranch? When she was going to be so sad? Why'd you beg her to stay? And then turn bitter when she didn't?"

His dad's brow pinched. "What do you mean?"

"You always told me Mom didn't want to ranch, but that you convinced her she'd eventually love it. If you hadn't pushed her—"

"We used to tell you that story because it was true.

Mom was a city girl. I did convince her to live here with me, to marry me, and she *was* happy."

"What? Mom was never happy here."

His father's features etched with anguish. "She was. When we were first married, she tried gardening. Canning. She got involved at church and began to feel connected. She did love it here, at first. But then…" Dad's fingertips dug into his closed eyelids. "But then she had Autumn. After, she struggled through some depression. It looked like she was going to get better, but when she got pregnant with you, it sent her into a downward spiral again. We tried so many things to help her. So many doctors. Medications. Prayer. Therapy. Nothing worked. It was like she'd stepped into a darkness and I couldn't find her. Nothing I did helped. She pushed me away, and I let her. I didn't know what to do."

Hunter's thoughts scrambled over one another like puppies in a pen. "But I always thought… I always thought that she'd given up her life for us and that it had broken her. That she'd been so despondent because you'd convinced her to marry you even though it wasn't what she'd wanted."

His dad's sigh was as long as the decades of hurt between them. "No, that wasn't the issue," he continued, voice quiet. "The story we used to tell you was true. I did convince her. I knew I couldn't live without her, but she was content here for a while. Until her illness. But you are right to blame me. I wanted to help her and I failed." His father pushed up from the wooden chair. Walked to the window. "I was so confused. So lost. I wrote her a letter once, thinking maybe since I was so bad at telling her how I felt, that writing it would help. Would remind her how much I loved her, no matter what."

The letter Hunter had found. Hunter couldn't believe his father was bringing it up.

"But then, like a fool, I didn't give it to her."

What?

"Maybe if I had told her more often how much I loved her. How much I wanted her here…maybe it would have made a difference."

"What do you mean you never gave Mom that letter?"

His dad's gaze snapped to him, filled with a heat that seared across Hunter's skin. "You knew about it?"

"I found it once when I was younger. It looked as though it had been read over numerous times."

His dad studied his hands and cleared his throat. Took a few seconds to steady his visually cracking composure. "I read it over the years. Punished myself with it after Mom left. Regretted not giving it to her. Being young and immature wasn't an excuse. I'd been prideful."

The creases in his dad's brow multiplied. "By the time I wrote that letter, she'd begun to take out some things on me. I didn't know what was happening. I just thought she didn't love me any longer. And so, instead of fighting for her, instead of giving her the letter or telling her how I felt, I let her go. I let her slip away one day at a time. I'll always regret it. I should have fought for her. I should have given her the letter and hundreds more, no matter how she was treating me or what I assumed she thought about me. I was hurt and wounded and I let it affect my decisions. It was so hard to lose her when we'd once been so happy. Watching her suffer and not being able to fix it. The more she struggled, the more I broke, too."

Hunter wanted to harden his heart against this man he'd never understood. But his grasp on that anger was slipping into sorrow. His father hadn't turned angry and bitter because his mom hadn't stayed or because he'd fought for her and lost, but because he'd never fought at all.

The opposite of everything Hunter had ever believed. Pain pounded in his temples. He'd been such a jerk to Rachel, and his actions had been based on false conclusions. How could he have been so foolish?

All of this time, Hunter had been wrong. He'd been self-righteous, assuming he knew what was best for Rachel. Driving her away from him when all he'd wanted to do was battle to keep her—even if he didn't know what that would look like. Why couldn't they date like she'd suggested? Why couldn't they have had an adult conversation and figured things out?

He'd been such an idiot. At this point, she must hate him. He'd hidden his true feelings from her—which sounded a bit like the story unfolding in front of him.

Hunter had always thought his dad was a jerk to his mom. That he'd ruined her life. But his dad had just been hurt and confused, and he'd done his best with a wife who'd changed. Who'd had an illness that nothing helped. Compassion for his father flooded him for the first time in his life. His dad wasn't to blame. Had never been. The man had held himself accountable all of these years for his mom's decline, and Hunter had been only too happy to join him in heaping on the guilt.

Hunter finally understood. Could finally forgive.

The question was, would Rachel ever do the same

regarding his mistakes? The wall around her that had taken most of the summer to break through was back up. And if he knew her at all, she didn't have any plans to ever let it down again.

He pulled out a chair and dropped into it. "This changes so much. I didn't know…didn't understand." His dad's red eyes broadcasted the grief their conversation had induced. "Dad, I'm so sorry."

"For what? You didn't do anything wrong."

"For all of it. I should have…" Asked sooner. Had more faith in his father instead of blaming him.

"Me, too, son. Me, too."

Chapter Sixteen

During her first week in Houston, Rachel had accomplished very little except going to work and heading home to Dana's apartment at night. She was supposed to be hunting for a place to live. She was also supposed to be happy.

Dana had forced her to go out to dinner last night, and she had perked up a bit.

Until she'd crawled onto the couch and tried to sleep. She'd never been so exhausted in all of her life, yet was unable to find any rest.

Rachel walked to her Jeep in the school parking lot, the heat and humidity thick like warm, sticky Jell-O. It was Monday. Mondays were good for lists and plans. She'd hoped today was the day excitement over getting her dream job would kick in and she would stop thinking about Hunter.

Hadn't happened.

Instead, she'd had three parent meetings at school. What had they all been about? Getting their kids into Ivy League universities. None of their children showed any interest in that very thing, but parents were lining up at her door.

Rachel had taken this job so she could help students. She hadn't realized so much of her interaction would be with their parents. She'd assumed it would get better once school started and the kids were on campus. But when she'd broached that question today with her supervisor, she'd only confirmed Rachel's worst fears. It seemed at this school, parents were always going to take up a large chunk of her time.

And she was afraid that wasn't the only reason she couldn't find any joy in the job she'd wanted so badly. She missed her people back home. And home itself. But what was she going to do about that now? It was too late. She'd made a decision, and she needed to stick with it.

Her phone rang, muffled in her purse, and Rachel dug for it.

Val.

She wasn't going to be disappointed that Hunter's name didn't appear on the screen. Was not. And in that same vein, she also didn't miss his texts. Or his voice. Or the way he teased her constantly and made her laugh.

Rachel didn't miss any of those things.

She swiped to answer, infusing perkiness into her hello.

"Hey, I thought you'd be at work and I'd have to leave a message."

"Just walking out."

"I have some news for you."

"What about?"

"Hunter. Do you want to hear it? Or are you content as can be down there?"

Air leaked from her lungs. "I'm...not unhappy." But wasn't the opposite of happy exactly that?

Rachel unlocked her Jeep and got in, then started it and cranked the air-conditioning, trying to combat the heat that had swelled as the vehicle roasted in the sun all day.

"Hunter said something to me yesterday that I haven't been able to get out of my mind. He asked me about you. Asked how you were."

"He did?"

"Yep. And when he did, I said, if you're so concerned about Rachel, why'd you push her away? To which he replied, 'This was her dream.'"

What? "What does that mean?"

"I'm starting to think the reason Hunter reacted the way he did isn't because he doesn't care, but because he does."

A flutter started in Rachel's chest and she broke into a sweat. She adjusted the vents to pummel her arms and face with crisp, cool air.

"Then why would he say those things to me?"

"So that you'd go. Tell me this. How confident were you that he felt something for you—a lot for you—before he sent you packing?"

At times she'd wondered what he was thinking, but mostly Rachel had listened to her heart and observed the way he treated her. Deep down, she'd known that he had to feel something for her. "I didn't really doubt it." Not with the way he'd protected her and watched out for her. The way he was always there when she needed him. And his kisses...

"Maybe he didn't want to be the reason you didn't take the job. Did you tell him how badly you wanted it?"

Rachel's eyes closed. "Yes." A ten, she'd told him.

Not even a sliver of a doubt. And then, in the police car that night, he'd encouraged her. Told her how amazing she would be at it.

"If he did this because of what you're saying, without telling me how he feels, then I want to hunt him down and hurt him." That immature teenage girl inside of her always popped up at the worst times. Perhaps, just perhaps, God would prefer she choose the less violent route.

"I know he never told you how he felt, but I could see it. We all could. And when you took the job—"

"Without talking to him first," Rachel continued Val's thought. She'd done the same thing to him. Pushed him away. "I self-sabotaged. I accepted the job without telling Hunter about it in order to protect myself. Yes, I still wanted it, but I was also scared that he might not love me the way I love him."

Love him. It had rolled right out, that truth. She should have known. Should have admitted it sooner. "Taking the position was a way to escape without finding out the truth. Because it would have hurt if he didn't feel the same. It does hurt. I'd assumed I'd learned this lesson watching Cash with Liv—that I was open—but I wasn't. I was running, protecting myself all along."

Rachel had also believed that the job would make her happy. Climbing another mountain, accomplishing another something. And for what? To prove she wasn't a troubled kid anymore? Who did she need to prove that to, besides herself? And she already knew the truth. God didn't have a list of things she had to check off in order to be forgiven or to start fresh. Her slate had been wiped clean yesterday. It would be wiped clean today. Same tomorrow. He loved her exactly as she was. Even the friends and family surrounding her loved her like that.

She'd thought the town had been waiting for her to mess up. But now? She was afraid it had all been her. Her judgments against herself. Her fears. It was time she learned grace didn't keep scorecards.

"I'm an idiot."

"You're not an idiot." No matter what mistakes she made, Val always had her back like a protective mama bear. "You were doing your best. And if you think there's a chance for you and Hunter, then there's something else I need to tell you."

Val proceeded to shatter Rachel's world further by telling her about the guidance counselor position at the high school in Fredericksburg, suggesting Rachel check into it. But even after they'd finished the conversation and Rachel had driven back to Dana's apartment, her mind was muddled.

It would be one thing if Hunter had wanted her to stay. Or he'd called to tell her about the job. But she and Val were simply guessing his feelings. What he'd told her—how he'd acted—wasn't anywhere near what they'd just discussed. And Rachel wasn't sure she could put herself out there again. She *had* attempted to talk to Hunter before moving—it might not have been the perfect scenario, since she'd already taken the job—but she'd tried discussing how she felt. And he'd shoved her away. The pain of that washed over her all over again. Felt like she was walking around bleeding for all the world to see.

Rachel could finally admit she loved Hunter. Always had. Always would.

The question she didn't have an answer to, was what she was going to do about it.

* * *

On Friday evening, Hunter stood outside Rachel's apartment door in Houston—make that her friend's place—and readied for a fight.

It had taken him a few days to process all his dad had revealed to him and to pray over his next steps, and he'd come to a very simple conclusion: he wanted Rachel in his life, and he'd do anything to make that happen.

His fist went up, then paused before connecting with the wooden door. *Wuss.* Hunter had thought about bringing Moose along for moral support—he'd known the dog would have pulled on Rachel's heartstrings and might have edged the score in his direction—but he hadn't wanted to force the animal to endure such a long drive in his truck.

He knocked, the sound reverberating in the pounding in his chest, and tried to run through everything he wanted to say.

The door flew open, revealing a much shorter woman than Rachel with dark hair and chocolate eyes.

"You must be Dana." He attempted a smile, but his nerves probably made it look like a wobbly spaghetti noodle. "I'm Hunter. Any chance Rachel's here?"

Recognition flashed on Dana's face, and she looked over her shoulder and called out, "Rachel, someone is here for you." Then she opened the door wider and motioned for him to come in. Bustling over to the kitchen counter, she grabbed a brown leather purse. "I was just… heading out." She bolted through the open doorway, then paused. "It was great to meet you." The nicety was followed by the sound of the front door slamming shut.

Huh. Was her departure a good or bad sign?

"Who is it?" Rachel came out from the bathroom,

and at the sight of him, froze. She must have recently come home from work, because she still had on business clothes. Slim dress pants that landed just above her ankles and a flowing shirt. The turquoise color highlighted the green of her eyes. Her hair was down, and her feet were bare, the heels she'd likely taken off when she'd walked in the door haphazardly lying to his right. Her toenails were painted fluorescent pink. Hunter had never imagined he could actually miss something like knowing Rachel's current polish color.

She glanced around the living room and kitchen. "Where's Dana? You didn't add breaking and entering or kidnapping to your list of crimes, did you?"

Strangely enough, the sassy question alleviated his tension. Just being near her made him feel like he'd taken his first real breath in almost two weeks.

"She just left. Said she had to be somewhere."

Rachel's closed off body language told him her walls were up and functioning. On high alert for anyone who tried to breach them.

"What are you doing here, Hunter?"

She was beautiful, inside and out, and he'd been so stupid not telling her how he felt.

"I need to talk to you about something."

"You could have called."

"This wasn't a phone call kind of conversation." Besides, she wouldn't have answered. Didn't she realize he knew her better than that?

She shifted uncomfortably. "Okay."

He strode forward, hands landing on her arms, her skin soft and smooth to his touch. "I'm so sorry. Sorry that I let you go and that I didn't tell you I was crazy in love with you and always have been and not one thing on God's green earth is ever going to change that."

Whoa. That hadn't come out exactly as he'd rehearsed. Her jaw had gone slack, and he was almost certain a sheen of moisture appeared in her eyes. She blinked so fast he could be wrong, though.

When she didn't say anything in response, he stormed ahead.

"I have a whole long story that might help my behavior make more sense." He pulled her over to the couch and motioned for her to sit. Then he sat on the coffee table across from her and told her everything. About how he'd always thought his dad had convinced his mom to live a life she didn't want—and how that turned out not to be true. He explained how it had messed with him over the years. How it had convinced him to never ask anyone—including her—to stay in a life she didn't want. He told her about the letter. About finding out that his father had never fought for his mother.

"I wanted you to come to Houston because I knew this was a dream of yours and I didn't want to take that away. And that's still true. I can live without a ranch. But I can't live without you."

"What are you saying?" Her voice was a whisper, her eyes questioning. Still aching with hurt that he'd caused.

"I'll move here if you're willing to give us a chance. I'll work in a hardware store. Or on a ranch outside of town. We can do long-distance if you want, but that's only going to last for a little bit. And then I don't want things to dead end. So if we want a future together, I'm willing to move. I still want you to follow your dreams. I already talked to my dad. Told him I might need to sell back to him. He understands." His father had been so decent about the whole conversation that Hunter had almost checked for hidden cameras. But then his dad had sent him out of his office with a gruff "Get to work," and Hunter had known he was still in the right universe. The two of them were both making more effort in their relationship, though, and things were slowly changing.

"This is probably all coming out jumbled, but I'm trying to explain why I didn't fight for you. Why I let you go. I thought it was the best way to love you." He let out a slow exhale. "But I don't believe that anymore."

"What do you believe now?" Her voice was still quiet.

"That I love you and I want to spend the rest of my life with you and I'll do anything to make that happen."

She popped up from the couch and began pacing.

Not exactly the response he was hoping for.

After four turns, she paused in front of him. "It's not going to work for you to move here."

A boulder of disappointment crushed him.

"That wouldn't make sense because I'm not going to be living here."

What? What was she talking about? "Is something wrong with your job?"

She nodded. "It's not at all what I expected."

His heart drummed so hard he was certain he could feel it tapping against his rib cage.

"I'm sorry." And he was. He wanted her to be happy. Hated hearing that she wasn't. Yet, at the same time, hope rose up. "There's a position that just opened at the high school."

Her head shook. "No, there's not. They filled it."

How many times could his dreams be snuffed out in one day?

"From what I've heard, the person they hired is straight out of school. Young. Blonde." Her head tilted. "I should set you up with her."

He wasn't sure whether to sigh or growl or yell.

"Really? What's her name? I'll have to call her." Anger and sarcasm blended together, frustration causing his body to heat despite the cool air in the apartment. What was he going to do with this woman? How was he going to convince her that—

"Rachel Maddox."

Absolute silence reigned after her words.

And then he was standing, gripping her arms again. "You took the job? It was you?" She nodded, a smile inching across her face. "And you let me go on and on? Here I was thinking I might never be able to convince you to give us another chance and you'd already decided?" His voice had risen to a boom.

Her grin only grew. It was mesmerizing, but Hunter was doing his best not to let it distract him. He was mad at her. Or, at least, he wanted to be. She lifted one shoulder. "I thought you needed to grovel a little."

He scooped her up in a hug, and she squealed, her arms looping around his neck. "Hunter McDermott, put me down."

"Never." After not nearly long enough, he let her go slowly. She slid down until they were face-to-face again. "Does this mean you love me and can't live without me?"

Her lips pressed together, and she gave the sweetest nod he'd ever witnessed in his life.

"Say it."

She sighed and rolled her eyes, acting annoyed by his demand, but then she softened. Her eyes were so full of emotion that he knew what she felt, even without the words he couldn't wait to hear. "I love you. I'm never going to leave you. You're my home. And if Fredericksburg isn't right for me, you'll be the first to know." His breath caught. "And then we'll figure the next thing out together."

Every tense muscle in his body unwound. "You love me."

"At the moment. But you're really going to have to up your game, McDermott. I'm expecting flowers every day, and you're going to have to learn to cook, and—"

He cut her off with a kiss. It seemed like a good plan. One he'd need to use again in the future. His hands slid into her hair, the pain of the last two weeks ebbing away at the familiarity of her touch. He could just stay right here forever. Except…he needed info.

Hunter managed to wrench himself away from her, holding her at arm's length. "How did you know about the job? Val?"

She nodded. "I interviewed with the high school on Wednesday and they offered me the job right away. But then I had to decide what to do. I didn't want to leave my current school hanging, but I talked to my supervisor, and she understood my predicament. I guess she reads romance novels all the time, and she was almost giddy about us. I told her I wasn't sure we were going to work, but she encouraged me to take the risk. The person who was in line behind me for the job here hasn't found anything else yet, and they're going to offer him the position."

He tucked back a piece of her hair, and if his hand lingered against her cheek, sue him.

"I didn't know what you were thinking," Rachel continued. "Or how you felt about me. I only knew your actions showed me something completely different than your words, but you definitely threw me for a loop. Val told me what you'd said at church and we pieced together what we thought was going on." Her face grew serious. "But I was still scared. I wasn't sure what to believe anymore. So I prayed, and I asked Val and Cash and Liv to pray, and in the end…taking the job in Fredericksburg was the right thing to do. And so I decided to trust God with that—whether you wanted me or not."

"I want you."

At his words, a smile traced her lips. He barely refrained from kissing her again. But he needed more reassurance. He had to know she wasn't giving this up for him. "I thought you loved the city. You know how different it is. Are you sure?"

She traced soft circles with her thumb across the scar on his forearm—a gash that had required stitches a few years past. "I don't have any doubts. Ever since my parents died… I've felt like I didn't belong anywhere. Colorado was a pit stop. I made friends but never got too close. And even though I was starting to love it in Fredericksburg, I didn't let myself believe it could be home again. Leaving last time and going to school was the right thing to do. But that doesn't mean it's the answer this time. That quiet life I never thought I wanted… I was wrong. I already have a home. I just had to open my eyes to see it."

Relief was as sweet as lemonade on a scorching day.

"I was fighting against letting people in. Belonging. And I don't want to fight that anymore."

"So you won't hate living in Fredericksburg, let's say…on a ranch?" At his question, her eyebrows shot up, and he felt a full-fledged grin growing. "I mean, not that anyone is asking you to live on a ranch." Yet.

Her lips curved. "Because that would be a crazy idea."

Inching closer, he slid arms around the small of her back. "Absolutely crazy." And wonderful. "Have I told you I don't love you today?"

That earned him a laugh.

"That works out well, then, McDermott, because I don't love you, either." Her arms wrapped around his neck and tugged him down until her lips met his in a soft kiss. "Except I do."

"Me, too." And he liked the sound of her last two words a whole lot.

Epilogue

Rachel peered out the window of Mr. McDermott's home to the rows of white chairs lining the west side of the house and facing the ranch. A white tent lit with twinkle lights stood to the right, waiting for the reception to follow.

The ceremony was about to start, so everyone had taken their seats. Olivia was holding Ryder in the front row. The Redmonds were seated behind her, and across the aisle, Hunter's dad sat with Autumn and Calvin, who was holding their newborn son, Craig.

Rachel's favorite aunt and uncle had made the trip from Austin—her Aunt Libby had been a huge help with wedding planning. And some other friends from town were there, too—ones who had known her since she was a kid, and much like Hunter, stayed in her life through all of her ups and downs, mistakes and triumphs.

If there was one thing she'd realized over the last few months about the man she was about to marry, it was that his love for her had been consistent. Hunter had always known exactly who she was—even beneath any bad decisions she'd made—and he'd loved all the sides of her. He'd always believed in her. It was mesmerizing to watch his adoration unfold now that he no longer had to hold back. She could say without a doubt that his love had changed her for the better.

Bree and a small group of teens sat toward the back. After Rachel had returned to town, Bree had begun to open up again, even attending the Bible study that Rachel led one morning a week before school. Between that and stepping in as Olivia's new assistant volleyball coach when Val's mom retired from the position she'd held for many years, the last few months had raced by.

Rachel and Hunter had planned their outdoor wedding for early November—the weekend after volleyball season ended—knowing full well it might be raining or freezing and they'd end up doing the ceremony in the tent. But like a little smile from God, the day was gorgeous. Trees were brandishing their royal colors, and the sun had come out to play in all its glory.

The front door of the house opened and her brother stepped inside. "They're almost ready for you."

She abandoned the window she'd been peeking out of to meet him by the front door. The guys were wearing crisp, dark jeans, white shirts and camel vests—with cowboy boots, of course. Hunter had opted for the casual look—Rachel couldn't imagine him donning a tux—and she had no doubt her soon-to-be husband was going to look heart-stopping in the ensemble.

"You look really nice. Almost worthy of that beautiful wife of yours. I'm not sure I've seen you this cleaned up…maybe ever."

Cash jutted his chest out, tugging on the front of his vest. "I wore a suit for my wedding."

"That's true." Amusement traced her lips. "You did."

She adjusted his orange calla lily boutonniere, which had slipped to one side.

For wedding colors, Rachel had opted for pops of orange, red, yellow and green. Val and Brennon were standing up with them, and Val had been tasked with the job of picking out her own bridesmaid's dress. She'd chosen a sweeping yellow one-shouldered dress that dropped to the floor with all of the drama the girl herself didn't possess. Perfection.

Rachel snagged her bouquet bursting with brightly colored calla lilies from the table by the front door. It looked amazing against her white, A-line, sleeveless dress. She eased her hem to the side, drinking in the sight of her shoes. Bright, bold green peeked back at her. She'd done her hair in a low side twist, opting not to wear a veil but to tuck in a sprig of greenery, instead.

"You look beautiful." Cash interrupted her love affair with her green satin, peep-toe pumps, and she found him looking at her with unguarded emotion that almost sent her free-falling down the same slippery slope.

"Thank you."

"I'm sorry Dad's not here."

"Me, too." Her eyes misted. "But I'm really glad you're here."

His creased cheeks spoke volumes. Of silent grief and the subsequent bond that flowed between them. "Me, too. Are you ready for this?"

"I am."

"So you really like this guy, huh?"

That got a laugh out of her, and the nerves that had started at seeing all of the people arriving calmed. "You know, I kinda do."

"And to think, only a few years ago I was working

on letting you go. That whole saying about releasing things so they'll come back to you is true."

Humor tugged on her lips. "You're a dork."

"Aaand that sounds more like the sister I know and love." He grinned. "Have I told you how proud I am of you?"

"Not this week."

"You should be proud of yourself, too."

"I am. I think." Rachel had been working on letting go of needing to prove herself and trusting that God's opinion—His great love for her—mattered more than the past, present and future jumbled together. And she was happy in this town, with her family and friends, and with the man about to become her husband. She'd had no idea she could be so content with what she'd been fighting against for so long.

Music drifted through the open door, and Rachel placed her hand in the crook of Cash's arm. They made their way outside and down the front steps. About forty chairs were filled with guests for the simple ceremony they'd timed to start just as the sun began to set.

When they reached the end of the aisle, Rachel sought Hunter's gaze and found it wrapped around her as if no one else existed.

Lands, she loved him.

His dimples sprang to life as if her thoughts had been spoken out loud.

She and Cash walked down the aisle as Grayson hopped on one foot up front, impatiently waiting to perform his job as the ring bearer, and Kinsley, their precocious flower girl, twirled in her white dress, both of them making the guests titter with suppressed laughter.

Gray had been full of questions about his important role for weeks. Though Rachel did think she'd convinced him that having a spider on the ring pillow was not the best idea.

Pastor Greg did the whole who-gives-this-woman part, and then her hand was in Hunter's and she was standing face-to-face with him.

"Hi."

His whispered greeting made her mouth curve. She was pretty sure they weren't supposed to be talking except to say their vows.

"You look…" His eyes filled with emotion, and he paused to swallow, causing his Adam's apple to bob. So, of course, the waterworks sprouted for her, too.

"Do not make me cry on my wedding day, Hunter McDermott."

That playful grin of his returned. "Yes, ma'am."

The ceremony went by in a blur. Rachel only knew she'd promised to share her life with someone she never wanted to live without. She was good with that decision.

"I now pronounce you husband and wife." Greg's head tilted toward them, his voice low. "Who knew that when Lucy Redmond suggested the two of you help with the float, we'd end up here?"

Rachel's mouth dropped open. Hunter's head shook in answer to her silent query, his cheeks creasing.

"I didn't know, either."

Both of them glanced in Lucy's direction. She was sitting with Graham and her girls, absolutely beaming from the second row. Guess Rachel would have to thank her later for her meddling. Laughter bubbled in her throat. Leave it to Lucy to quietly stick her nose into their business and come out looking like a shining star.

Greg eased back, speaking in a louder voice. "Hunter,

you may kiss your bride. And in case anyone is wondering, this is *not* a first kiss."

Laughter rang out, along with a cheer from their friends and family, as Hunter's lips met hers, his arms warm and strong around her. His whisper cascaded by her ear. "Time to head back down that aisle as a married woman, Mrs. McDermott." He inched back to look into her eyes. "Need a lift?" He made a motion, almost bending, as though he planned to scoop her up like he had before.

Her eyes shot to the size of dinner plates, and she whacked his shoulder in front of God and all of the guests. "Don't you dare!" The words hissed out and were met by a low chuckle as he straightened. Winked.

"I wouldn't dream of it. At least, not on our wedding day. But after..." He shrugged as if to say he couldn't control the future.

Her huff of exaggerated annoyance was negated by the smile that accompanied it. "What have I gotten myself into?"

"Only the best decision of your life, darlin'."

For once, she agreed with him.

"Ready?" He offered her his elbow, and she linked her arm through his as they faced the people who loved them and took their first step into the world as husband and wife. She couldn't wait to do life with Hunter by her side. Tears pricked her eyes as she contemplated the amazing man God had written into her story. He was more than she'd ever hoped for, a rock when she needed it, and most of all, he loved her with a devotion she almost couldn't understand.

She might not deserve him, but she planned to keep him.

* * * * *

If you enjoyed this story,
pick up these other books by Jill Lynn:

FALLING FOR TEXAS
HER TEXAS FAMILY

Available now from Love Inspired!

Find more great reads at www.LoveInspired.com

Dear Reader,

Rachel was a broken teen in *Falling for Texas*, and I was so excited to write a redemption story for her. But as it goes in life, sometimes our best-laid plans get disrupted.

Between books two and three (this one), I lost a friend to cancer. Before she passed, we wrote a book together. After, I had a hard time writing fiction again. I went round and round with Rachel and Hunter's story. Finally it all came together. But I felt a lot of pressure to get it all right. To complete it. To do it on my own instead of crashing into Jesus and trusting His timing.

I am the type, like Rachel, who wants to write my own redemption story. As if I can work hard enough or earn enough grace to cover my mistakes. Which, of course, is the opposite of the definition of grace.

Rachel struggles to show everyone she's changed. And she has. But she forgets that she's already loved and forgiven. That human judgments don't count. Only God's opinion matters. The moment Jesus gave up His life on the cross, her redemption story (and mine and yours) was completed.

I love to connect with readers. Find me at facebook. com/JillLynnAuthor or at instagram.com/JillLynnAuthor for conversations about life and God and everything in between.

My newsletter is where I send out announcements about upcoming books and sales. Sign up at Jill-Lynn.com/news.

Jill Lynn

With his orphaned nephew depending on him, Amish carpenter Eli Troyer moves to Harmony Creek Hollow to start over. And when schoolteacher Miriam Hartz offers to teach hearing-impaired Eli how to read lips, he can't refuse. Given both of their pasts, dare they hope to fit together as a family...forever?

Read on for a sneak preview of
THE AMISH SUITOR by *Jo Ann Brown,*
available in June 2018 from Love Inspired!

"If you want, I can teach you to read lips."

"What?"

Miriam touched her lips and then raised and lowered her fingers against her thumb as if they were a duck's bill. "Talk. I can help you understand what people are saying by watching them talk."

When he realized what Miriam was doing, Eli was stunned. A nurse at the hospital where he'd woken after the wall's collapse had suggested that, once he was healed, he should learn to read lips. He'd pushed that advice aside, because he didn't have time with the obligations of his brother's farm and his brother's son.

During the past four years he and his nephew had created a unique language together. Mostly Kyle had taught it to him, helping him decipher the meaning and context of the few words he could capture.

"How do you know about lipreading?" Eli asked.

"My *grossmammi*." She tapped one ear, then the other. "...hearing...as she grew older. We...together. We practiced together. I can help." She put her hands on Kyle's shoulders. "Kyle...grows up. Who will...you then?"

Who would help him when Kyle wasn't nearby? He was sure that was what she'd asked. It was a question he'd posed to himself more and more often as Kyle reached the age to start attending school.

Not for the first time, Eli thought about the burden he'd placed on Kyle. Though Eli was scrupulous in making time for Kyle to be a *kind*, sometimes, like when they went to a store, he found himself needing the little boy to confirm a total when he was checking out or to explain where to find something on the shelves. If he didn't agree to Miriam's help, he was condemning his nephew to a lifetime of having to help him.

"All right," Eli said. "You can try to teach me to read lips."

Miriam seemed so confident she could teach him. He didn't want to disappoint her when she was going out of her way to help him.

Kyle threw his arms around Miriam and gave her a big hug. He grinned, and Eli realized how eager the *kind* was to let someone else help Eli fill in the blanks.

Don't miss
THE AMISH SUITOR by Jo Ann Brown,
available June 2018 wherever
Love Inspired® books and ebooks are sold.

www.LoveInspired.com

LIEXP0518